THE
MALTESE
KITTEN

A SAM THE CAT MYSTERY

SAM THE CAT MYSTERIES

SAM THE CAT: DETECTIVE

THE BIG CATNAP

THE MALTESE KITTEN

FOR INFORMATION ABOUT THESE TITLES
please contact:
CHESHIRE HOUSE BOOKS
P.O. Box 2484, New York, New York 10021
or look for Sam's web site:
HTTP://WWW.SAMTHECAT.COM

THE
MALTESE
KITTEN

LINDA STEWART

CHESHIRE HOUSE BOOKS
NEW YORK

CHESHIRE HOUSE BOOKS
P.O. Box 2484
New York, New York 10021

COVER ILLUSTRATION: Sam Ryskind

DESIGN & PRODUCTION: Bernard Chase

ISBN 0-9675073-8-3

LIBRARY OF CONGRESS CATALOG CARD NUMBER
2002113091

THE
MALTESE
KITTEN

A SAM THE CAT MYSTERY

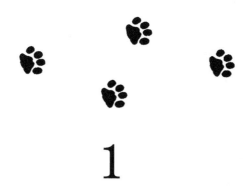

1

I was on a Missing Persian case and prowling around Soho. This was not the case of the year. His ex-girlfriend, a disappointed Tabby, wanted him back, but when I found him, in a little Italian bistro on Lafayette, up to his whiskers in antipasto, he was eager to stay unfound; so I didn't find him and walked away.

It was nearly ten-thirty on a freezing December night. The radio, the last time I'd heard it, predicted snow, and by the time I got back to 11th Street the moonlight was full of dots. I paused at the corner and crossed at the light.

My agency office (a Mac and a phone) is a little one-cat operation that I run out of Hunnicker's Bookstore. I entered the bookstore and angled my head. From the darkened hole of the rear office, Otto Hunnicker's raspy voice, prerecorded and stuck to tape, was explaining "Hours from ten to six. If you leave a message, I'll call you back."

I raced to the office. Mostly the calls that come in the evening are meant for me and I expected the jilted Tabby.

"Aren't you back yet, Sam?" It was Sue.

I jumped to the blotter and pounced on the Speaker. "Yeah, I'm back," I informed her. "Just."

"Are you cold and hungry?" she said.

I grinned. "Is that an offer?"

"An offer to what?"

"To fix me dinner and keep me warm?"

I could hear her bristling over the phone. Whenever she bristles, her whiskers twitch and she does me this thumpety thing with her tail. "I was only kidding," I said. "I'm sure you're much too busy to—"

"Sam, be quiet. There's a girl here who wants to see you. Her name's Miss Wonderful."

"Yeah I'll bet. You think she's a customer?"

"Likely so. She went to your office and said you were gone so I told her to wait for you. Her and her lox."

"She brought me some—"

"That, and a spoonful of caviar, Sam."

I pictured it—black as sin and corrupt with the scent of Iranian waters.

"Send her in, darling. Send her in."

Sue was calling from right next door where she does the night shift at Kitten Kaboodle—a kind of combination beauty parlor, boarding house and boutique—a word she tells me is French for "rip-off." Sue's a buddy and maybe more.

I took a second to clear my head and clean my

2

whiskers and lick my paws and take my seat in the swiveling desk chair. Then I tried an appropriate face: piercing eyes and a savvy grin. Or savvy eyes and a piercing grin. I was still deciding when Miss Magnificent popped through the mail slot and cat-footed in.

I watched her come on to me, hearing that faint, provocative click of stiletto nails as she angled her way through the darkened bookstore. She got to the office and moved with a slow and sinuous subtlety into the light. She was totally slink and the color of tea—*hot* tea and forget about lemon, this one was strictly sugar and spice, and she stood in the doorway and frisked my intentions with much too adorably innocent eyes.

I said, "When you're ready."

She said, "Do you bite?"

I said, "On occasion, but never a client."

She nodded approval and leapt to the desk. "Then I'd guess you could handle yourself with a villain?"

"You got any villains?"

"I'm hoping I don't."

"That's good for a starter," I said.

Her eyes were a nearly miraculous turquoise blue and she knew how to handle them; yes she did. She lowered them prettily, melting the desk. "It's so hard to continue," she breathed, "I'm not... I'm not even sure where I ought to begin."

I said, "The beginning's the natural spot."

"That's at 9:47," she said.

"Uh-huh."

"He got the phone call at 9:47. He said, 'I see. From my ad in the Post?' And then he said, 'Yes.'

3

And then he said 'No.' And then he said, 'Yes, I can bring him tonight. To the Beaumont Gallery? I know where it is. At ten-thirty? That'll be fine.' And then he— oh Mr. Sam, Mr. Sam!—" the eyes were anguished; the paws were tense— "he just suddenly grabbed Little Fluffer and left!"

I said, "Uh-huh. And then who's Little Fluffer?"

"Why Little Fluffer's my only son! Oh I know what you're thinking. You're thinking, my goodness, she doesn't look *nearly* old enough to have children, but Little Fluffer's a total infant. I mean he's only eleven weeks old. And he's such a sweetie." She tested a smile. "And such a beauty. He looks just exactly like my dearly departed husband."

"I'm sorry to hear that," I muttered. "I mean— I'm sorry to hear that your husband's dead."

"Oh he didn't die, dear. He simply departed." She flicked her shoulders and added, "Men!"

I didn't go near it.

"He's also Maltese. I believe as a kitten he came here from Malta. My mother warned me. She said, 'Miss Wonderful, once a rover, a rover again.' But we never listen—I mean to our mothers. So now I'm a widow." She looked at her feet.

I waited politely. "The guy on the phone—"

"He's my human roommate," she finished. "John. Mr. John O'Shaughnessy."

"Yes. I see." And the actual fact of it was, I saw. I'd seen it too many thousands of times. Human roommate dispatches kitten. He calls it adoption. I call it a crime.

"Did he leave with a carrier?"

"Yes. He did. It was purple canvas with yellowish straps and a sort of an—Oh!" She looked up at the window. A hovering shadow tapped on the pane, then raised its head up and said, "I'm sorry. I didn't think you were—"

"Spike! Come in." I could see the sparkle of snow on his shoulders, the icy dots on the ebony fur as he leapt through the window and thwunked to the floor.

I turned to Miss Wonderful. "This is Spike—my upstairs neighbor and sometime assistant. Spike—Miss Wonderful."

Spike didn't speak. He stood there and gawped at her, cocking his head. His ears were rigid. His eyes were bright. His curving mouth formed the shape of a Wow.

I said, "Miss Wonderful's here with a case."

"You can call me Brigid," she cooed, and tossed him a jeweled look from those gaudy eyes. It came close to killing him.

"Brigid," he managed, and made a spontaneous leap to the desk as though he'd been fired from a loose cannon. "It's not too serious, is it?" he mooed

She nodded somberly. "Yes. It is."

I said, "Her roommate went off with her son. He put an adoption ad in the paper and somebody bit from the Beaumont Gallery. She wants me to go there and rescue the kid." I looked at her quickly. "Is that about right?"

"Oh yes, exactly," she said. "Can you do it?"

Instead of an answer, I frowned at the clock. "We've only lost about twenty minutes. You said they were meeting at, what— ten-thirty?"

Again she nodded.

Spike took a breath. "We'll need a description,"

5

he said, "of your son." I shot him a questioning look at that "we" but he didn't notice it. All his attention was focused on Brigid— watching her face and contorting his own in an idiot's grin. "Would you say he's a beautiful redhead like you?"

"He looks like her husband," I offered.

"Ex," she announced to him quickly. "And sort of like you. He's tremendously handsome," she purred, and dealt him another blow from those killer eyes.

"Are you saying he's black?" I intruded.

"Yes."

"Distinguishing marks?"

"Um...not that I know of."

"Not that you know of?"

"He doesn't have marks."

"And his eyes are—"

"Green. They're sort of a...green."

"Uh-huh." I nodded. "And where should I bring him?"

"Where should you bring him?" She frowned and looked thoughtful. "Well I guess...could you bring him here? I mean if I waited at Kitten Kaboodle?"

I shrugged indifference. "It's fine with me. There's the matter of payment," I prompted.

"Yes. I left a deposit with Sue next door. She put it on ice for me. Oh! I see. You mean if you find him, you'll want—" She sighed. "How much will it come to?"

"The usual cost for a rescued kitten is half a pound."

"You mean British Sterling?"

"And don't play the goof. I mean Scotch salmon. Or Nova Scotia. In cases of hardship, I'll settle for lox. Plus, of course, expenses."

"Oh dear. I see. But I'll have to be frank with you, Mr. Sam. I'm a single mother. I'm not even sure I can get my paws on another fish. But oh if you find him I'll give you a backrub and tickle your tummy and—"

"Say, it occurred to me," Spike interrupted. "If Sam's too tired—" he shot me a glance— "and you do look tired— been out all day and you must be exhausted—" He looked back at Brigid. "I thought I could, well—with your lovely permission, I'd give you a discount and do it myself."

I leaned back and watched them. Brigid The Wonderful eyeball to eyeball with Spike The Enthralled.

"Oh Spike, could you really?" She flashed him a smile that you could have read newspapers by. "That's sweet. And you wouldn't be frightened?"

He batted the air. "I'm a trained detective. I'm never frightened. Come on, Miss Brigid, I'll see you safely to Kitten Kaboodle and then I'll be off."

He held his paw up.

She giggled and rose.

"I'll show you a shortcut," he said, and motioned her up to the window and out to the night.

I pivoted slowly and angled my head. I didn't like it. I liked her lox, but that's where it ended. Her acting stank, and her general story was more full of holes than a cashmere sweater in moth heaven.

I did what I had to and counted to ten.

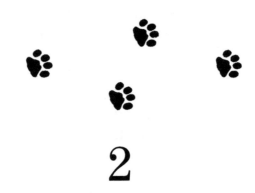

2

At the count of seventy, Spike was back, popping up at my window like noisy toast.

"Finished already?" I chirped.

He opened his mouth and closed it but didn't speak.

"It must've been grueling," I pressed. "I mean, if you'll pardon the comment, you look so tired. Did you have any—"

"*Stop!*" he exploded. "*Please!*" He remained at the window and lowered his head. "All right, I apologize, Sam. My behavior was really disgusting. In fact—I'm a worm."

"I was thinking pig," I announced, "as in greedy."

"I was thinking worm," he appealed, "as in low."

I considered the option. "A piggy wormlet's a reasonable compromise. What do you say?"

He pawed at his whiskers. "Well...now I don't know. I was kind of leaning towards wormy piglet."

"Wormy piglet," I said, "is okay."

He leapt to the blotter. "I truly apologize, Sam. I just— I don't know what happened. I looked at those eyes and got carried away."

"But not quite as far as the Beaumont Gallery?"

He looked at the carpet and mumbled "No."

"Was there any reason?" I said, without mercy. "A trained detective—"

"C'mon! Let up! I didn't get to the Beaumont Gallery."

"Because?"

"*I didn't know where it was!*"

"It's on Fourth and Chameleon," I offered.

"Sam? How did you know that?" He narrowed his eyes.

"I'm a trained detective." I flicked my tail at the open phonebook. "I looked it up."

If you work in Manhattan, and if you're a cat, the easiest place you could manage to work would be Greenwich Village— a patch of turf that's south of 14th Street and north of Houston (pronounced as House-ton, but never mind.) What you get in the Village is relative quiet, and minimal traffic, and cobblestone streets, and three-story houses, and street-level shops, and meandering alleys, and gated parks with the kind of gates you can slip right under or jump right over and poof! you're gone.

The dislikable thing that you get in the Village is total confusion. Irrational routes. Triangular streets that appear out of nowhere and bend like a hairpin and end in a knot, so, for instance, 12th Street traverses 4th Street and sends you in circles at Abingdon

9

Square.

It wasn't exactly a night to get lost. It had stopped snowing and nothing had stuck but the streets were deserted and glistening wet and a boisterous wind, coming straight from the river, was drumming up tunes on the garbage can lids.

We'd gotten to 4th Street and stopped for a light. It was one of those corners that wasn't a corner but more like the meaningless point of a V, and it offered a starburst of possible streets. I spotted a penny and said, "Want to flip?"

Spike shook his head at me, shivering deeply and trying to bury himself in his coat. "Angle a right and then cut through the garden."

I looked at him briefly and said, "Are you sure?"

"I'm freezing to *death*," he announced. "Am I sure?"

I nodded agreement and followed his lead.

We walked in silence.

"I dated a girl once at Seven Chameleon," he said. "Bernadette. She worked at a shop called The Fatal Fedora."

"I beg your pardon?"

"The Fatal Fedora. It's one of those shops that sells poisonous hats."

I said, "Spike, will you stop it?"

He started to laugh, and his laughter sat there, like smoke in the air.

"What they sell there is magic," he offered. "Tricks. Invisible inkwells, and some of those cute little wiggly spiders you pull out of—"

"Right. So what did she do there?"

"She sat in the window and flirted with tourists,

10

is what she did. You know. She'd see one and leap at the window and do little mewings and angle her head? She could rope in the suckers like nobody's business."

"You're sounding bitter."

"So maybe I am. She ran off with a mouser," he said. "A sneaky, no-good Persian with muscles for brains."

"But you learned your lesson."

"Oh yeah. Of course." He looked up at me sideways. "So what did I learn?"

"Not to act like a sucker," I said. "And not to go out on a limb for a flirt with a face."

"You're referring to Brigid," he said.

"You guessed."

We were crossing the garden, a brave little plot that was taking the winter with vegetable spunk. The grass was spiky but hanging in. At its further edges, the frozen lamplight floated like vapors of yellowish fog and surrounded a sign that said *4th and Chameleon.*

I hit the sidewalk and glanced at the street. The Fatal Fedora was shut for the night but its neon intelligence winked at the world: *"Tricks Can Be Treats,"* it instructed in yellow, and burbled in purple, *"It's Fun To Be Fooled."* It was number Seven. We wanted Twelve, so we kept on trucking.

The street was dark, with no other shop lights and no other lamps. If the buildings were houses, then no one was home. I noted a panel-truck parked at the curb with a hand-lettered sign that said *Beaumont Gallery/ 19th C. Art and Antiques.* It was parked at Eleven. We trotted to Twelve where a darkened

11

window— a giant bay— showed a couple of paintings, a grandfather clock and, beyond its horizon, a darkened room.

"So we must've just missed them." Spike looked relieved. The grandfather clock said 11:11. I looked for an entrance. A bit to the side was a trio of steps that led down from the sidewalk and killed a few feet till it got to a door.

I went up to the steps and looked down at the door. There was nothing special about that door. It was just a door like a million others, with wooden panels and one of those knockers that looks like a lion who's eating a bagel.

"I'd like to go home now." Spike sounded firm. "Let's get outta here, Sammy. It's locked for the night."

I nodded agreement and still didn't move. There was something eerie that came from the building. The kind of silence that comes from a grave and it fixed my attention and tickled my ears.

I went down to the doorway and sniffed at its hinge. The aroma of terror came out with a force that was practically physical. Punch-in-the-nose. It was partly human and partly cat, and whatever had frightened them reeked of cigars.

I motioned to Spike. "C'mere for a second. I need to borrow the tip of your—"

Nose, was the end of that sentence, but just as I thought it, the wind cut me off with a hideous shriek like a chorus of witches who wanted their supper and wanted it *nowww!* It banged at the knocker and rattled the door.

I turned at the rattle and jumped at the *pop!*—

the sound of a bolt blowing out of its cradle and hurled myself forward, bombarding the door with the flying propulsion of all fours.

I must have been lucky. It suddenly gave like a grandma at Christmas. The thing busted inward, and carried me with it, and whanged at the wall.

I dropped to the carpet and motioned to Spike, but before he could make it, the wind double-crossed me and doubled behind me and suddenly—*SLAM!*

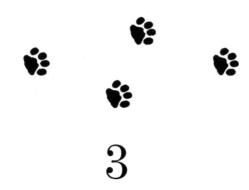

3

There wasn't time to think about doors. A man's body was flat on the floor. It lay on the carpet, its polished shoes pointing up at the ceiling, its face to the side, and its Burberry overcoat buttoned and sashed.

The showroom itself was of medium size and was showing some paintings and elderly clocks and occasional tables and rickety chairs. Along towards the back was the door to an office. No one was in it, or so I presumed, which left me with Burberry, dead or alive.

I gritted my teeth and then sniffed at the carpet that led to the body. I smelled the cigar, and the hesitant paws of a terrified cat, and the odor of cinnamon mingled with sweat.

The sweat and the cinnamon rose from the body. I paused beside it and glanced at its face, which was one of those faces you wouldn't glance twice at unless it was lolling around on your floor. It was pasty and pudgy, and say about forty, with one of those noses that looks like a blob.

I walked from its head to the tip of its loafers, a probable distance of five foot and change, and looked down at its fingers, which hadn't been fighting, scratching, poking, or picking its blob, and observed that its watch-face had smashed on the carpet. The fall had stopped it at 9:42.

At the back of the office a telephone rang. It sounded shrill and a little lonely and died abruptly, leaving its small, disappointed ghost in the silent air. I went back to the body and circled its hairdo— a lousy comb-over job stuck with glue but with no indication of blows to the noggin. No other bruises, or none I could see, and a second sniffing— a check for gunpowder, blood or poison— had nothing to say except "Cinnamon-cinnamon." Hardly a help. I mean what could have decked him? A stale Danish?

I pawed at his cheekbone and found it warm, but it didn't mean much. I reached for his throat and explored for a pulsepoint. Instead what I found was a half-buried needle. It sprung from his neck like the thorn from a cactus— a cinnamon thorn— with a yellowish feather attached to its tail. So that was the answer. Someone had drugged him. Someone had lobbed him a sleepytime dart, and as though to confirm it he snorted and groaned.

Okay, he was living.

I breathed some relief and then sat on the carpet and sucked a few nails. I could look for the kitten, or look for the cat, or examine his pockets. He snorted again, and I went for his pockets, extracting a fine-looking Cartier wallet with inches of cash and the

15

gilded initials of *SLB*. A few wallet-sized photos fell out on the floor: An elderly fellow in front of a sign that said *Beaumont Nursery, Wigham, New York,* and the jerk on the carpet with several cats and a goofy expression. I dug for some more. A package of breath mints. A cellular phone. A plastic credit card, notably bent. A traffic ticket from Wigham, New York that was dated last evening at 9:53, and indicted a Beaumont, Sebastian L. for exceeding a hundred and running a light.

Okay, that was something. I didn't know what, but the motive to shoot him had not been his cash and had probably not been connected to kittens, which meant that the kitten was probably here.

I yelled a soprano-ish, "Heeeeere, kitty-kitty!" I sounded creepy. The kind of a voice that you'd tell your children to run from and hide, so I tried a more dignified, "Here, Little Fluffer!" which got me an answer I didn't expect.

"Little Fluffer's been kidnapped." Spike shot his head through the door to the office. "C'mere. Get a load."

I looked up at him, squinting. "You want to explain how you—"

"Got through the window? Sure. It's a snap. It gives out on the alley. I happened to know that particular alley from La Bernadette." He jerked at the Burberry. "What's with the bod?"

"You mean Sleeping Beauty?" I said. "She's alive."

"Is it Brigid's landlord?"

"Nope. It's a Beaumont."

"You think he's the owner?"

I shrugged. "I don't know."

I got to the office and gawped at the scene.

There were fingers of glass where the window'd been busted, and somebody's footprints had blackened the sill. On the floor by a closet was Beaumont's luggage—purple canvas with yellowish straps and a dangling dogtag with "*SLB*." On a desk in the corner—a 7-foot table that held a computer, a lamp and a phone—was a matching carrier, neatly unzipped and disturbingly empty.

"Kidnapped is right." I leapt to the window and sniffed at the sill. Whoever the cat was who'd been on the carpet had been at the window. A male, about eight, but the rest of his odor was swamped by cigar. "Did you check out the carrier?"

Spike shook his head. "And besides, what's the difference? I mean if he's nabbed—"

"—we should know what he smells like. Come on. Do it fast."

We got onto the table in daredevil leaps— me, from the window and Spike from the floor, and we skidded and skated. The surface was slick, and the slippery slick smelled of lemony polish, with essence of Beaumont and stinky cigar, but the pit of the carrier gave something else. Something milky and fishy and slightly acidic and certainly fluffy and totally scared. Whoever'd been in there was shedding a bucket— the lining was lousy with ebony hairs, and a few had been caught in the teeth of the zipper.

Spike looked it over and waggled his head. "So somebody yanked Little Fluff from his carriage and left by the window."

"He left by the door."

17

"Why not by the window?"

"Why not by the door? He came in by the window. He stood in the office and shot Mr. Beaumont—"

"You mean with a *gun?*"

"I mean with a dart-gun. The angle's perfect. Beaumont was bullseyed and dropped like a stone. The intruder examined him— leaving his odor surrounding the body—and walked out the door, where he stunk up the doorway."

"I see what you mean." Spike thought it over. "*And*—" he said brightly, "he didn't slam it. The lock didn't catch, which is how come it opened!"

"A brilliant idea."

"I suppose if it's brilliant, you thought of it first."

I was planning to lie and allow that I hadn't but destiny spared me. The telephone rang. It rang at my shoulder which caused me to jump since it rang like a siren in search of a fire, and it caused Mr. Beaumont to rouse from his funk.

"Muzza-muzza-ma*zuzz*-a?" he puzzled. "Wuzza?"

We leapt to the window and out to the icy, dicey dark of the empty night.

4

New York, New York. It's a wonderful town. Something along the lines of an Oz without the music, but with lots of wizards and witches. Everyone's got a shtik. It's a city driven by money and powered by envy, so color it green. If you're looking for motives, it's one or the other—envy or money— or frequently both, so I thought about motives: *Why steal a cat?*

I was back on Chameleon and freezing my tail. Spike had gone south at the Beaumont alley. Spike's got a roommate and has to get home before Donna The Roommate arrives and goes ape, which is why he won't make it. Not as a dick. A successful detective is always a loner. He's one of those cats that survives on his own—without any roommates, without any strings. He keeps his own counsel and keeps his own score. He's at home in a world where he's always a stranger. It's never a picnic, this stranger's world. It's often tragic and sometimes funny—at least in the way of a horse's laugh or the rasp-berry sound of a Bronx cheer. But down these green streets a cat must go who is not himself green, who's experienced at his job and has a natural taste for the hunt.

I was hunting a witness, and way out of luck. The street was empty—the houses were dark and the shops were as closed as a principal's mind.

I stopped in the sheltering cove of a doorway— *The Gypsy Tearoom & Astral Boutique*, it said on the awning— and tried to get warm. I'd got to the corner of Pork and Chameleon. The rest of Chameleon, the block to the north, was just as deserted as everything south, and it looked as though Pork was as quiet as ham.

I turned and looked up at a sound from the window—the sound of a whisker that tickled a wall— and found myself staring at opaline eyes. They belonged to a Calico stretched on the sill. She gestured "C'mere." I gestured a "How?" and she flicked at the doorway that offered a wide and appeal-ing mail slot. I jumped at the chance.

Inside, it was eerie. The walls, painted black, had the signs of the Zodiac painted in gold, and a cluster of tables with Zodiac cloths. My hostess awaited me, right near the slot. She inspected me coldly and nodded twice.

"You are wanting info," she said. Her accent was mildly Hungarian.

"Yep. That's a fact."

"Have a sit on my table," she said. I followed her up to a table and sat near a vase with some paper azaleas. She eyed me again. Her face wasn't young but it seemed to be ageless. Her body was plump, and she'd lost a few teeth, but she didn't much smile so it didn't much matter. "Your name would be...?"

"Sam."

She agreed with me. "Yes. And you come to my tearoom," she noted. "Late, but is better than nitchky, so please to relax. Madam Lazonga is telling you all."

"Madam Lazonga?"

"This would be me."

"I'm delighted to meet you. Perhaps you could tell me—"

"I already told you. I'm telling you all. I'm revealing the secrets, I'm spilling the beans, I'm reporting whatever. I say what I see and I see what I'm saying."

I nodded. "Uh-huh. So my question is—"

"Why you are seeking a pawist?"

I thought it over, which wasn't a help. "Well you got me stumped, lady. What's a pawist?"

"A pawist's a pawist. I'm reading your paw. I'm telling you voyages, strangers and money. I'm reading your nails and I'm telling you love. Like a palmist for humans, a pawist for cats."

I nodded politely." Except that my questions are more—"

"Be silent!" she said. "Is vibroxy! Madam Lazonga is going in trench."

"I beg your pardon?"

"Madam Lazonga is closing her eyes, is pronouncing an *Ummmmmmmmm.*"

Madam Lazonga was doing just that. What she meant by a trench, I decided, was trance, and she did it theatrically, thrumming an *ummmm* like a carnival diva at Carnegie Hall. She opened her eyes and said, "Please to give paw."

I decided to do it. I gave her my paw and I started to blather. "I'm sure you can see I'm a private detective," I said.

She nodded. "A private detective is written like ink. It's the first thing I notice." She frowned at my paw with supreme concentration.

"And second to that, that I'm seeking a kitten."

"A *cuddly* kitten." She tapped at my paw with a dagger-like nail. "Here it says 'cuddly,' "— she zig-zagged her nail to the tip of my elbow— "and here it says 'cute.' "

"You are truly amazing."

She nodded. "I know."

"And you've certainly noticed the kitten was stolen. You probably know it was done by a man who came out of the Beaumont—"

"You're talking the gallery?"

"I'm talking the gallery at nine-forty-five."

She looked up at me sharply, her jaw in a gape. "But I'm actually saw this! With actual eyes!"

"That's terrific!" I blatted.

"No-goodnik!" she snapped. "You are *double* no-goodnik! Get out of my house!" She flung out her paws and displaced an azalea that flew off the table.

"But Madam," I said, "I was *hoping* you'd seen it."

"Of course you would hope. But I'm seeing in window not seeing in paw. If I'm seeing in window, I'm not getting paid and you're not telling neighbors I'm wonderful-smart, and I'm starving and dying and this you would hope? You are *triple* no-goodnik!"

I gave her my paw.

She suddenly brightened. "You wish me to read?"

"I would very much like it."

She settled her rump on the Zodiacked table and took up my paw. "Mmmm....Mmmm-*hmmmmmmm*-hmmm. Now. Let me see....Uh-huh, uh-*huh*. You see here he is walking, is holding a fuffle."

"A fuffle?"

"A bag. Is a kind of a bag what you call it a fuffle."

I said, "You mean duffel?"

She peered at my paw. "Here it looks like an *f*," she said, shrugging indifference. "Is anyway yellow and jumping around. It goes wiggle and jiggle. He's giving it potch and he's telling it—"

"Potch?"

"Punch?"

"Punch!" I said, nodding. "Go on."

"So he's giving it potch and he's telling it 'Sha!' So I'm thinking, Lazonga, what kind of crazy potches a fuffle and gives it a *Sha*? And I'm thinking what's in it? I'm not thinking kitten, I'm thinking a devil, I'm thinking a dog, but I'm now seeing kitten, I'm now seeing cat but it's little and tiny."

I nodded. "The man—did you see what he looked like?"

"So what's with the *did*? I am seeing this wonder-ful-clear in the paw. Over here I see skinny, and here I see tall, and right over here I see smoking cigar."

Bingo! If I'd had any doubts that the lady was riffing, I started believing. I prompted, "Go on. Can you see what he's wearing?"

"Is wearing peace coat and also wutchkiss."

I squinted. "Peace?"

"You know—like a sailor. A sailor-boy jeckel. The color of navel—"

23

"A pea coat!" I said.

"Nuh-Nuh-nuh-*nuh*-nuh! A jeckel like this, couldn't nobody make it from one single pea it would take you a plateful. Madam Lazonga is telling you four-hundred-seventy peas."

"And what's with the wutchkiss?"

"Up on his head like a little fadoodle. You make it from wool."

"Are you saying a watch cap?"

"That's what I said."

"I have one other question."

"Then give other paw."

"What's the matter with this one?"

"I already read. It's the end of the chapter."

I took back my paw and selected another.

"Continue with ask."

"Did you see where he went to?"

"*Did* ?" she said.

"Do."

"Madam Lazonga is seeing in paw. Madam Lazonga is seeing sailor-boy turning the corner. Is walking to Pork. Is passotsky by window where beautiful cat, being Madam Lazonga, is sitting on sill and is seeing exactly."

"Exactly...what?" I was growing impatient.

"Is entering doorway. Is entering doorway of ear being hot."

"Can you say that in English?"

"Doorway," she said, and put down my paw again.

What did she mean? I looked up at the window and peered at the street...and then suddenly got it.

"Madam, you're swell. So what do I owe you?"

"A fortune," she said. "You could never afford it.

You couldn't afford it you're working your tail off for seventy years. You can pay me in kindness."

"I certainly will. What kind of a kindness?"

"A fella like you has some hotsy and totsy society friends, you can throw me some business. You're telling them, 'Visiting Madam Lazonga gives pieces of mind.' "

"I'll be happy to, Madam." I leapt to the floor. "But I have to be honest. My friends aren't rich."

"But I see you will meet some," she promised me. "Soon. Three little princesses. One dozen paws. This is happening Sunday at possible noon—if you're living till Sunday," she added.

"Madam?"

But Madam Lazonga was back in her trench, and the sole explanation she offered was *ummmmmmm*.

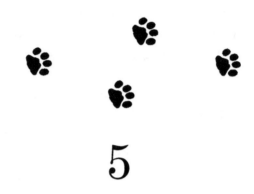

5

The Pearl Hotel was as seedy as grapes. Eleven stories of soot-covered, weather-eroded brick with a neon sign that had barely managed a dimly flickering EAR HOT . I pushed my way in through revolving doors and into a lobby with ratty carpets and plastic couches and dying palms and nobody in it except for a night clerk, a guy in his eighties who snored at the *Times*. On the counter beside him, a ferret-faced Rex lay on top of the register, chewing his tail. I leapt up in front of him.

"Beat it," he said. "We ain't got a vacancy."

"Yeah. Sure you don't. All the crowned heads of Europe are booked for the month.—Have you got a new guest here?" I offered him.

"Beat it."

"The question," I told him, "is multiple choice, and the possible choices are 'yes' or 'no.'"

He looked up at me cunningly. "Sorry there, Mac, but the possible choices are beat it or scram."

This was just what I needed. A creep on the make-out at one in the morning.

I swallowed my tongue and then sighed at him sorrowfully. "Gee, what a shame. The guy said if I found him, he'd give me some shrimp."

"Shrimp?" He was interested. "What kind of shrimp?"

I consulted the menu. "Your favorite kind."

"You mean fried?" he said.

"Fried." I leaned over and whispered, "I'd give you a cut if you help me to find him. It oughta be worth about... twenty percent?"

"Outta how many pieces?"

"A hundred and twelve."

He scratched at his noggin. "So how much is that?"

"You mean twenty percent of it? Gee, I don't know. But I bet there's an adding machine in your office."

He glanced at the office— a darkened door at the side of the counter, and said, "I'll be back."

He jumped to the carpet and raced to the door.

"Take your time," I yelled after him. "Math's pretty hard."

I opened the register, warm from his rear, and then looked at the entries: A "Peter Patter" had checked in this evening at 9:48.

Okay, that was perfect; in fact, on the nose. He was "Peter Patter" like I'm Peter Rabbit, but even his alias gave me the clue that whoever he was, he was not Mr. Strictly Legitimate Citizen.

Now what? I thought. Now I needed his room number. Where would it be?

I looked up at the night clerk who snored like a dog, and then carefully, silently, not even clicking my nails on the marble, I walked past his bulk and then jumped down beside him, in back of the counter.

A voice from the shadows said: *"Hold it right there!"*

The voice wasn't kidding. I held it right there.

"Now turn around slowly," it added, "and point those paws at the ceiling."

I stiffened my spine.

He said, "Turn around slowly and—"

"Stick it on ice."

"I beg your pardon?"

"I don't roll over for crummy hotel dicks, so—"

"Stick it on ice? I suppose you mean cool it," he said. "You wise-guys are swift with the patter. All right. Turn around."

I pivoted slowly and looked at the gaunt and intelligent face of a brown Siamese. "What's your name and your business—" he gave it a growl— "and spare me the whoppers."

"The name would be Sam and the business is private."

He stared at my face. His eyes were that weary and watery blue that had seen about everything, possibly twice, but they weren't unfriendly. They simply inquired.

"Meaning private detective," I added. "Listen— we're in the same business. I'd been in your place, I'd've done the same movie-lines."

"Yeah, I suppose. And if I'd've been you I'd've called myself crummy." He held out his paw to me. "Brutus," he said, "but my friends call me Buster."

28

"Then Buster it is. Let me tell you my problem. I'm after a guy who I think took a room here as Peter Patter."

"You do gotta love it," he said. "The idiot names they come up with. So what'd he do?"

"Seems he kidnapped a kitten."

"The miserable lug! He's in Room Thirty-Seven, if that's what you're after."

"That's what I'm after. You see him come in?"

"Sorry, pal. I was elsewhere. He isn't the only rat in this flea-bag. Or even the only flea in this rat-bag." He scratched at his chin. "You are not at The Plaza, in case you're confused. I did hear him squawk, though. He phoned to the desk. Said his window was sticking, his room was like ice, and he wanted a bottle."

"He get it?"

"The booze? Oh yeah. Got delivered. Of course, Mr. Fritz—" Buster jerked at the night clerk— "got gin for himself, so it's bye-bye to dreamland. He'll sleep through the shift."

"And who's his assistant?"

"You gotta be kidding. Assistant? Around here?"

"Then who was the Einstein with spit on his chin?"

"The kid on the counter?" He shrugged. "I dunno. He said his name's Wilmer. He came off the street so I said he could stay here until he got warm. He's not on the payroll, if that's what you mean.— Where is he?"

"I'm here!" Wilmer yelled from the office. "And twenty percent is a hundred and twelve."

"I think you're mistaken," I yelled. "Try again."

29

Buster looked at the office and waggled his head. "C'mon," he said quickly. "I'll show you the shortcut to Room Thirty-Seven."

I followed his lead.

The "shortcut" turned out to be a trip through an open window, into an alley, up to the top of an upended mattress that leaned on a wall, and from there to the rungs of a fire escape ladder.

The metal was slippery. The ladder was cold, and the wind from the east blew at fifty an hour. It was one of those nights to be home on the rug, not patrolling in alleys, but this is my life and I happen to like it.

We got to a landing, a metal balcony spanning the width of a couple of windows—both of them curtained and bouncing the moon against battle-scarred windowpanes, blackened with grime. A woman was sobbing in one of those windows. I pictured the tears getting into her ears as she wetted the pillow and wept through the night. In the other window, a man and a woman were having their argument: "Harry," she spat, "if you weren't so cheap, we'd'a stayed someplace decent."

Buster kept climbing. I followed his tail, jumping over a mitten that lay on the step, till we got to the balcony one story up. Again, it was fronted by two dirty panes. "The one on the right—" Buster pointed— "is empty. This'd be Patter's." He pointed ahead.

We moved to it softly. From somewhere behind it, a hard, dirty light tumbled out from a strip about

three inches wide where the window was open—
presumably stuck there, as Patter had said. The wind
channeled through it—occasionally lifting and whip-
ping the edge of a dirt-colored shade.

We lowered our heads and then peered through
the strip. In the brown-yellow light of an overhead
light bulb, a bad-looking character slept on the bed.
A bottle of whiskey was clutched in his hand.
It seemed to be empty; its lip, pointed down at the
moth-eaten carpet, was dribbling air.

"So that's Mr. Patter," I muttered.

"Peter Patter is pickled," Buster pronounced.

He was also a string bean— a long, skinny guy
in a forest green sweatsuit, with yellow-blond hair.
His pea coat and watch cap were hung on the door-
knob.

I shuttled my eyes through the rest of room. On
the top of the dresser, I spotted the duffel bag— open
and empty. Beside it, a bowl with a puddle of water.

"Is that for the kid?" Buster jerked at the water.

I shrugged. "I don't know, but I don't see a
kitten."

"Describe him."

"He's black and he answers to 'Fluffer.' "

"Let's see if he does."

We lowered our heads to the slit in the window
and hollered out, "Fluffer! Here, little man!"

Nothing. Not a peep. Not a peek. Not a stir.

We tried it again and again nothing happened.

It wasn't worth trying to get through the
window—the opening was barely the size of my
head—but I wriggled my nose in and sniffed at the sill.
Then I sniffed at the underside edge of the window. I

looked up at Buster. "The kid got away."

Buster did the same sniffing. "I smell him, all right. He was up on the sill and he squeezed through the opening. So where does that leave us?"

I sniffed at the slats on the fire escape landing. The scent wasn't there. Any traces of Fluffer were gone with the wind.

"The poor little fella." Buster looked sad. "I don't think he can make it. Not on his own, and not in this weather. We'll give it a look but I'd—"

"Hold it a second!" The wind had come in from another direction and zapped me a clue. I said, "What does that smell like?"

"I don't want to know."

"Come on. Seriously, Buster."

"Seriously, Sam? It smells like a shrimp that got tossed in a sewer and drowned by a cockroach and ate by a rat and then barfed in a dumpster."

"Exactly," I said. "And the can that it comes in says 'Healthier Pet.'"

We moved to the odor, which led to the right and then up to the ledge of that second window and into the bowl of a half-empty can with a popped-open pop-top that rattled and rolled.

"'Healthier Pet,'" Buster read from the label. "'Shrimp-flavored soya with broccoli and kale and organic alfalfa.' Oh brother," he said. "I don't even want to *read* that, let alone eat it."

I said, "You're not kidding. Imagine pulling a stunt like that on an innocent kid. He must've been starving."

"The poor little guy. Even lost a few hairs in it. See? Little blacks?"

I examined a glop of the left-over gravy and looked at the sad little cluster of hairs. "He was lured through the window," I figured. "Somebody came up the ladder and flashed him the can."

"Or *down* the ladder."

"Nope," I said, "up. The guy shucked his mitten on one of those stairs on his way to the kitten."

"All right, Mr. Holmes. Why'd he take off his mitten?"

"To open the can."

"That's a nifty assumption but—"

"Nope," I said, "look." I flipped up the pop-top and showed him the ring that you pop the thing up by that gleamed in the light. There were dark woolen threads in it. "Now— wanna bet they're the same as the mitten? The guy tried it first—"

"When he still had his mittens on. Sam—you're an ace."

We went back to the mitten, which offered us zip. It was brownish and fuzzy and missing some threads but it held no aroma and nothing at all in the way of a label. We sat on the steps and exchanged a few groans and a pause full of thought.

"So I'm totally clueless," I said at the end.

"Well, you know he was kidnapped."

"And kidnapped again."

"The first time by Patter—"

"The second by...X."

"Yeah. Good ole X." Buster suddenly shivered.

"And not only that, but I've also got Y."

"Y being...?"

"Why are they after a kitten? I'd say Mr. Patter does not need a pet, and I'd say Mr. Mitten—"

"Does not need a kitten?"

I nodded. "Precisely."

"I see what you mean."

We shared some more silence.

"I'd better get going." I sat for a time and then stretched as I rose. "Can I ask you a favor?"

"You don't even have to."

"You'll watch Mr. Patter?"

"He won't make a move without Buster is on him like stink is on fish.— Let me know where to reach you."

I gave him my number and also my e-mail and wished him goodnight.

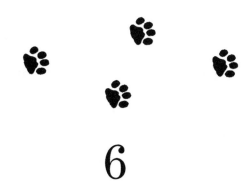

6

According to the same phonebook that had squealed on the Beaumont Gallery, John O'Shaughnessy, Brigid's roommate, lived at 6¼ Grove, about a block and a half from the Pearl.

Six-and-a-quarter turned out to be part of a cluster of houses you'd call "picturesque," meaning partially crummy, but crummy-antique. They were two-story houses, the kind made of bricks that had faded to pinkish with patches of white, and had little white shutters and little white doors, and they sat in a courtyard— a cobblestoned square with a tree in the center and houses for walls. The tree was a fir tree and one of the neighbors had gussied it up with some lights and a star and it looked pretty festive. I skirted the tree and got down to the houses. There seemed to be twelve— four in the center and four on the sides.

O'Shaughnessy's portion—the first on the left— gave me four little windows, which didn't much help, not with three of them darkened and all of them shut. The one with the lights on, at least, was convenient. A first-story job with an adequate sill and an absence of curtains.

I peered through the panes. On the opposite side was a "Tiffany" lampshade—a lit-up kaleidoscope perched on a desk that was pushed to the window. I narrowed my eyes and then squinted beyond it and into a room that was shadowy-quiet and totally still. A corduroy sofa. A small TV. A couple of bookshelves with plenty of books and a photo of Brigid asleep on a chair. I pricked up my ears and continued to listen:

Nothing. Nobody home.

I checked out the desk that was under the window: The back of an envelope, covered with scrawls. A couple of 3-for-a-dollar ballpoints with one of them missing and torn from the pack. A chain with car keys and some kind of medal. I wasn't excited. I squinted some more.

An old-fashioned typewriter sat at the side with a blank piece of paper arranged in its jaws that had two little words on it—

```
CHAPTER ONE
```

—and then inches of nothing. The paper was curled, as though no one had moved it since April was young, and it didn't seem hopeful that anyone would. On the blotter beside it, conveniently angled for easier reading, a typewritten page said

```
         McALLISTER'S GOLD
      The long-awaited sequel to
    the prize-winning novel MOONSHOT
                 by
         John D. O'Shaughnessy
```

36

Mr. O'Shaughnessy seemed to be blocked. I knew the feeling— that pain in the gut when the words didn't happen and thoughts don't arrive.

What arrived in their places, it seemed, were the bills. They were marked "Second Notice" and sat in a pile with a half-crumpled letter whose printed border said *Quibble and Quibble, Attorneys At Law* and began with the greeting:

EVICTION NOTICE

First: Whereas— it announced in italics (italics scare me as much as Whereas, which is why lawyers use them) *Whereas*, it proclaimed, *Your owner / landlord requires the use of your rent-controlled dwelling to use for himself...*

Well. No wonder the guy couldn't write. Getting evicted in Manhattan is getting evicted *from* Manhattan. There are simply no apartments here that anyone can afford. So in ugly truth, he was being deported. Banished. Exiled to the lap of the fruited plain where the coffee shops close at midnight and the copy shops close at ten. For most New Yorkers, this would be sad. For a New York writer, a special breed that hangs around Kinko's at 2 AM with a glazed donut and coffee-to-go, this would truly be torture; could even be death.

And what about Brigid? Would Brigid go with him? Or else would he dump her? Or else would she split? It was something to think about. Later. At home.

I was passing the Christmas tree, smelling the balsam and thinking of nothing, when suddenly— BLAM! They fell out of those branches like giant

37

cat-bombs and landed in front of me—three in a row. I examined them quickly: a trio of gangsters with alley-cat muscles and glistening teeth.

I froze and said, "Hi. So glad you dropped in."

The probable leader, a red Himalyan—a twenty-pounder with twigs in his fur, said, "We got us a joker." His voice was a rasp. It was something like gravel if gravel could talk and had something to tell you. "You wanna do jokes, I could give you the punchline." I ducked from the punch but instead it was verbal: *"Get offa the case!"*

"Case..." I said, frowning. "What case is that?"

The reedy lieutenants looked ready to pounce. The red Himalayan had lifted a paw, but then shook his head wearily. "Pally," he rasped, "you can stop bein' stupid or start bein' dead. The case with the kitten. The case that you're *on.*"

"That's the case that I'm dropping?"

"Exactly," he said. The paw settled down again. Both the lieutenants appeared disappointed.

"Who sent you?" I said.

"Who *sent* me?" he spluttered. "Nobody *sent* me. He thinks someone *sent* me," he said to his pals.

The yellow one snickered. The tabby collapsed in a fit of hysterics. "That's stupid," he croaked, "so it means we can kill him." He grinned at his boss. "Can we kill him now, Slasher?"

"Be patient, Magoo."

"But he thinks Mr. G—"

"Will ya button yer yapper?" The red Himalayan made sounds in his throat like he'd swallowed a motor. He growled at the thug and then rolled up his eyeballs and dropped them on me. "Just forget that he

38

said that."

"Forget he said what?"

"*Mr. G,*" he exploded.

"Why, Slasher," I said, "it's completely forgotten."

"And so is the case?"

I stared at him, frowning. "What case?" I said.

"You want I should eat him?" the yellow one offered.

The Slasher ignored him and stayed with my face. "I will try to be patient," he said. "*And patience is not what I'm good at.*" He lowered his voice and then swallowed more hardware. Again he looked up. "And so let us review," he said, practically crooning. "Now what did I tell you," he said, "to forget?"

"Mr. G," I said promptly.

He choked on a cog or perhaps on an axle. "You didn't forget! You're supposed to for*get* that I said Mr. G. What you're s'posed to re*mem*ber," he said, "is the case that I said to remember you're s'posed to for*get*! Are you gettin it, pally? It's not like it's hard. If you didn't remember the case to forget you'd forget to remember I said to forget it!" He glared at me. "Got it?"

I nodded. "I do. And I'm gonna remember it, Slasher. I will."

"*And don't you forget it!*" He showed me some teeth. "*Now scram,*" he said tightly, "*before I get mad!*"

7

There's a wonderful tree at the curb of the bookstore that's probably been there for seventy years. If it wanted to talk it could tell you stories—of flappers and rockers, of Edsels and Els, of radios playing on sweltering stoops when the voice of Sinatra was heard in the land and the Brooklyn Dodgers were whomping the Yanks. It might also inform you, though just in passing, that "newer" and "better" are not the same thing, and that stuff that comes later may not be improvements and things that are newer may not be as nice. I've developed a fondness for Hunnicker's tree, and I've watched it deliver its annual message—the message that winter comes later than spring, and yet in the springtime it's loaded with blossoms and here in the winter it's bare as a bone.

It was starting to snow as I rounded the corner. Billowy flakes did a dance in the air and the arms of my cherry tree seemed to reach out to them—

winter's blossoms; it welcomed them home. A larger blossom was perched on its branches: the idiot Wilmer, the Rex from the Pearl. He was watching the doorway with riveted eyes and he hadn't yet seen me. I U-turned around and went in through the courtyard and cut to my sill.

I stood for a moment and peered through the panes. A middle-aged customer paced on the desk. He was totally gray and exceedingly glossy. His ears were pointed, his eyes were green, and his coat was as smooth as a hummingbird's breast. The sum of his features, I thought, was Maltese, and he gave the impression of careful breeding, impeccable manners, and not much else. Around his neck was a lilac ribbon.

I leapt to the blotter and said, "What's up?"

He gave me the faintest of flickering smiles. "Are you Sam, the detective?" His accent was French but it sounded authentic.

I said, "Either that, or I'm robbing the bookstore. So what about you?"

"Do I look like a robber?"

"Mister," I said, "it's two in the morning, it's cold as a witch and I didn't invite you and yet here you are. If I didn't think 'robber' I'm not a detective."

He thought it over. "I see what you mean."

"Then start with 'Who are you?'"

"You're asking my name?"

"That'll do for the moment."

"My name is Jean-Clawed." He pronounced the thing *Zhon* but he Englished the Clawed.

"So how can I help you?"

He nodded and sat. He sat very nicely, arranging his body and folding his paws on the edge of the desk.

The drift of his odor was heavily sweet, as though he'd been dabbling in scented litter or been in a room that had strangled on Glade.

"It's a missing...item," he said. And then paused. "I am here on the part of its rightful...owner."

I took in his hesitance, measured his pause, and then nodded politely. "What item is that and what owner is rightful?"

"Be patient, Monsieur." He tested my patience by clearing his throat, adjusting his ribbon, and checking his feet. "If you help me to find it, Monsieur, I'm prepared to offer you five pounds of Maine lobster. Cooked to perfection, of course. Shelled. And with your personal choice of sauce."

I looked at him blankly and said, "Go on."

"May I now assume that I have your interest?"

"Five pounds of lobster's a lot of lobster."

"I was hoping you'd see it like that," he agreed. He was nervously playing around with a pencil. He batted it roughly— or roughly for him, and it suddenly rattled itself to the floor. He looked embarrassed. He said, "Forgive me, Monsieur," and leapt to the carpet to get it.

I looked at the window and studied the snow. He came up with a pistol, wearing the trigger like some kind of bracelet, and twirled it around. Its clear yellow barrel was loaded with ink.

"You will stay where you are," he said, sounding unhappy. "Your paws will remain on the top of the desk."

"And then what'll happen?" I stayed where I was with my paws on the blotter.

He dove to the floor. "I'll be searching your office

to look for that...thing."

"Well I'll be a monkey." I looked at him, laughing. "All right. Go on if it's giving you fun. Though it beats me," I said, "why you'd wait till I got here."

"A matter of timing." He poked through a bin. "The deplorable weather. My trip was delayed and I'd only just got here when, poof! you arrived."

"I don't ever arrive," I explained, "in a poof.— Why'd you think that I've got it?"

I watched as he walked into Hunnicker's closet. "It pays to make sure before spending one's lobster," he said from a shelf.

He'd of course left the pistol on top of the blotter. I spun the thing slowly and pointed it left. He came out of the closet and found it precisely and perfectly aimed at the loop of his bow.

"Now get yourself up here," I ordered, "and start making logical noises and cutting the pap."

"Good heavens," he said. "You don't have to get nasty." He trotted up quickly and leapt to the desk. "As I noted before, I'll be happy to pay you—"

"That five pounds of lobster."

"Exactly," he said. "For the speedy return of a certain kitten. An ebony kitten. With emerald eyes."

"And who are you working for?"

"Really, Monsieur. I am not free to tell you."

I shrugged. "Up to you, but I don't take a case with my head in a bucket. I need information."

"Then let us just say...that I work for the family. The kitten's family."

"You mean you're his father?"

"Most certainly not!"

"Then you work for his mother?"

43

"*Diable*! Not *her*!"

I looked up at the doorway. "And speak of the devil…"

She entered the room and then froze in the light. I gave her a wink and said, "Welcome, Ms. Wonderful. May I present Mr.—"

"Oh!" she said. "Him!"

I watched their reactions. An icy coldness had taken the room down to twenty degrees.

"So you've made his acquaintance."

"Of course not," she said. "Why I've never seen this man in my life."

I looked at the Frenchman. "She's lying," he said.

I looked back at Brigid. "He's lying," she said.

I grinned at them wolfishly. "Man, you're a pair."

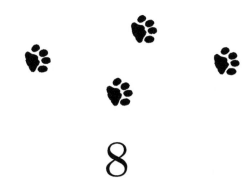

8

"If I follow your story," I said to Jean-Clawed, "you said you don't work for her."

"Not what I said." He looked over at Brigid, who sat on the Mac and pretended indifference. "Not that I do—I mean work for this...creature— but nobody asked me. You asked me, Monsieur, did I work for his mother. The kitten's mother is Fifi La Belle."

"And Fifi is who?"

"She's my seventh cousin."

"And Fifi is where?"

"I believe she's at home."

"It's like pulling hen's teeth," I said. "Where's home?"

"At the Beaumont Nursery. At Beaumont Farms."

I looked up at Brigid, who looked at her nails. "All right. I was fibbing," she said. "It's just that the truth is so...well...unbelievable, Sam. And I needed your help and I thought...well I thought you'd believe I'm his mother."

45

"I didn't," I said.

"You didn't?"

I laughed. "Not once you got talking. You talked too much, and you couldn't describe his distinguishing marks. And I never once met a genuine mother who couldn't recite every freckle and hair."

"But I'd swear you believed me."

I chortled again. "I believed in your caviar, kid, and your lox. Now suppose you start talking, and try talking straight."

She lowered her eyes and then swallowed some air. "My roommate," she said, "is just as I told you, a Mr. O'Shaughnessy." Now she looked up. "He's a kindly old gentleman. Seventy-three, with a sweet disposition. A heart made of gold."

"Uh-huh," I said flatly.

She gathered more wind. "Well the other morning, he went for a walk and discovered this kitten. I mean, on the street. I mean someone abandoned it, poor little thing. Well, his heart just went out to it—"

"Heart made of gold."

"—and he carried it home with him. 'Brigid,' he said, 'we must care for this kitten.' " Her voice had a throb and her eyes filled with moisture. "And that's what we did. Until yesterday evening. You see, he went out. I mean, Mr. O'Shaughnessy went to the market. And that's when the burglars came into the house."

I nodded. "The burglars."

"Yes! There were two! They came in through the doorway and burgled the kitten. Oh Sam, I was frightened. I mean I was just so entirely frightened, I hid in the tub."

"But you did get a look at them."

"Not very well. Like I said, I was hiding. But after they left, Sam, I ran to the window and watched them go off. They were driving a truck, Sam. And right on its side it said Beaumont Gallery, Art and Antiques."

She seemed to have finished.

Jean-Clawed looked amused. "That's the version she tried when she came to the gallery. I didn't believe it then and I still don't believe it now."

"So you work at the gallery," I said.

He nodded.

"And when did Ms Wonderful come with her tale?"

"I came about nine or so," Brigid threw in. "The kitten was kidnapped at 8:17."

I looked at Jean-Clawed again.

"Nine's about right. She came up to the window."

"And what happened then?"

"Nothing, Monsieur. I was there by myself. There was yet no kitten."

"So who brought him in?"

"Alas, I was napping, Monsieur. I don't know."

"But you saw Mr. Patter come in."

"Mr. Patter?"

"The guy with the dart and the lousy cigar."

Again he nodded. "I had to make use of a bottle of perfume to wash off the smell. Mr. B will be angry."

"Let's talk about P.—Had you ever seen him before?"

"Not at all. At least not till the moment he came through the window."

"He talk to Sebastian?"

47

"He stood in the doorway and spoke with his pistol, Monsieur. He said *Bang!*"

"And then what happened?"

"I happened to notice Sebastian's luggage was here on the floor and I noticed a kitten, Monsieur, a frightened little black kitten, in one of the bags."

"And then what happened?"

"And then I fled." He looked at the window, the fluttering snow. "If Monsieur will excuse me..." He started to rise. "We've completed our business. I'd better get home before snow overtakes me. You know where to reach me, Monsieur, if you like."

"By the way," Brigid offered, "I noticed a Rex in the tree by the gutter. You'd better watch out."

"A Rex?" he said, frowning.

"*The* Rex," she said. She looked at the Frenchman and lifted a paw and engraved an elaborate "G" in the air.

He nodded in silence.

"And speaking of G," I said, watching them closely. "He sent me some thugs." I described the three gangsters and mentioned their names.

Brigid looked startled. The Frenchman looked grim. He said quickly, "Excuse me," and leapt to the sill and then fled to the blizzard.

I watched him depart and then looked back at Brigid. She lowered her eyes.

"Oh for pity's sake trust me," she sobbed with a quiver. "I know I'm a liar. I know I've been wrong. But I need you so badly." She lifted her eyes. "I'm so...so... frightened and so...so...alone, and you're so...so..."

"Wonderful and brave?" I said helpfully.

"Oh yes!" she said. "Yes! Will you help me? Will you please, please help me?"

The telephone rang. She sat like a stone while I clicked on the speaker:

"Hey Sammy, it's Buster. Get over here fast."

"What's the matter?"

"Can't talk. Just get over here pronto." The phone went to static and suddenly died.

Brigid looked frightened. "Sam...?" she said

"Later. Go back to Kaboodle." I looked at the snow and then looked back at Brigid. "You'd best stay the night."

9

"Okay—there he is." Buster pointed his paw at a human-size bundle that lay in the snow. We were crossing an alley that butted the alley that bounded the fire escape wall of the Pearl, like the bend of an elbow. "I found him just now. When it started to snow, I got scared for the kitten and thought I'd go looking."

"And?"

"Not a trace. The guy isn't dead, by the way, he's asleep."

We got to the body: a sleeping giant in one of those windbreakers padded with down. At his side was a carrier, open and yawning and partly toppled and buried in snow. I circled the body and looked at his hands. One wore a mitten, the other was bare.

"I see why you called me," I whispered.

"No ID in his pockets." Buster looked up.

"Any darts in his collar?"

"Darts?"

I explained.

We examined the body, which didn't have darts but a prominent goose egg on top its head—a bad-looking lump with a crusting of blood.

Buster said carefully, "What do you think?"

I said, "Only the obvious. This is the guy.— So what about Patter?"

"He still hasn't moved. Hasn't even come to again. This fella here—" Buster pawed at the body— "he might've been out here for easy an hour."

I looked at the snow that had piled on his jacket and measured the depth of what covered the ground. It was several inches. "Or possibly more."

"So where does that leave us?"

I said, "Up the creek."

Whatever the clues might've been, they were snowed on. There wasn't an odor, a footprint, a crumb. I was getting discouraged, on top of disgusted, on top of distracted, on top of confused. I examined the alley. The side on the left was an empty building, a three-story house that was under construction, or *re*construction. Someone was building a patch on the roof and some pieces of lumber were stacked on the edge. On the opposite side were a couple of buildings with darkened windows.

End of the trail.

"So what're you thinking?" Buster said grimly.

"The same thing you are. The kitten was nabbed."

"Or maybe the kitten just kind of escaped?"

I thought it over. "Possibly yes. But considering everything, probably no."

"But anything's possible."

"Anything is."

"About those houses—" I pointed up at the darkened windows. "What do you know?"

"Not a thing," Buster offered. "The windows were dark when I got to the alley."

I nodded. "Okay."

I looked down at the man again. Reddish hair and the build of a linebacker. Nothing in that.

I went into his pockets again to make sure. Nothing was in them.

Buster was right.

The trail of the kitten was cold as the snow.

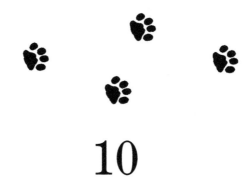

10

Sue waited up for me. Sometimes she does that, and almost always it knocks me out. Sometimes I say to her, "Susie, you shouldn't," and then she comes back at me, "Sam, shut up," so I know she's been worried, which knocks me out too.

I hit the corner and saw she was waiting— pacing the window that faces the street. Harry, the owner, had loaded it up with some catnip Santas and Christmasy lights but she lighted that window like nobody's business—a green-eyed redhead with me on her mind. Wilmer, the G-man, had left for the night.

As soon as I popped through Kaboodle's mail slot, Sue was all over me. "Sammy, you're wet and you're catching pneumonia. Come back to the couch."

I followed her silently, passing the sinks and the beauty shop mirrors and racks full of toys, and then into the "parlor," as Sue likes to call it—the little back room with the pink quilted sofa, the microwave oven, the desk and the phone. The sofa is plastic, so

Sue doesn't mind when I drip all over it.

"Here. Put *this* on." She tossed me a towel that she'd warmed on the heater. I ducked underneath it, inhaling its heat and the warm smell of Downy. She said, "Did you eat?"

"I believe I did once," I recalled, "in my youth."

"Why you poor little orphan," she said. "Can I fix you a nice bowl of porridge?" She flashed me some lox. It was Brigid's deposit, I gathered, still in its little Baggie and nesting on ice from a left over Pepsi.

"How is she?" I said.

"You mean Brigid? She's sleeping."

I glanced at the doorway that leads to the guest rooms and lowered my voice. "So what do you think of her?"

"Well...for a person who's totally gorgeous, I guess she's okay." She was moving the lox to a clean paper towel. "She's in desperate trouble, of course, but still, if you get past the trouble, she's basically...good.—Would you care for some capers?"

I shook my head no. "But where'd you get capers?"

"From Brigid, of course. She said it was caviar, Sam. It was capers."

I laughed sarcastically. "Yeah. She is good."

Sue didn't answer. She toted the lox to the arm of the sofa and said to me, "Eat."

We both started eating. The lox was superb. It was meltingly silky and pleasantly fat and we gobbled it silently. Lox doesn't lie.

Sue licked her whiskers. "Now tell me," she said. "I want to know everything. Start from the top."

54

I told her everything. One of those stories that goes on forever and doesn't make sense.

"But it sounds so hopeless," she said, when I'd finished.

"It can't be hopeless. It's Chapter Ten. There has to be more to it."

"More like what?"

"More to the story. Maybe the story's in why they're all after him. Why he's so hot. If I figured out Why, I could figure out Who."

"You mean who's got the kitten?"

"Or who'll get him next. For a wee little button, the kid gets around."

I scratched at my whiskers and stared at the wall. For a time we were silent.

"What?" she said.

"Nothing. I guess I was thinking."

"I know you were *thinking*," she said. "Thinking what?"

"That Brigid's a liar and Jean-Clawed's a twerp and it's making me crazy."

She gave it some thought. "So you mean he's not lying?"

"Except by omission. He's just not saying what needs to be said. But the lady's a liar. She said so herself."

"But she's not lying *all* the time, Sammy. I mean she lives with O'Shaughnessy. That much is true. And she didn't imagine the Beaumont Gallery, and then there's the kitten, who's certainly black, and the purple carrier, just like she said. You know? Like you found in Sebastian's office?"

I angled my head at her. "So? What's your point?"

"Well it's just like the lox and the caviar, Sammy. Like half what she says could be perfectly true."

I looked at her levelly. "Right. Which half?"

She thought for a second and nodded. "Oh. So it's still like a guessing game, isn't it."

"Yep."

"So what're you guessing?"

I rolled to my back and then stared at the ceiling. I stared for a while. "I'm guessing," I said, "that he's Fifi's kitten. I'm guessing," I said, "he was born on the farm and then stayed with his mom till he learned a few manners and somebody suddenly brought him to town."

"You think Brigid's roommate?"

"I've no idea. But it doesn't strike me that Mr. O'Shaughnessy needed a kitten right now in his life."

"You mean getting evicted and all. Okay. So what if he found little Fluff on the street? Like the way Brigid told you."

"And *then* what?" I said. "Do you think he 'just happened' to call Mr. Beaumont? I didn't see posters around on the street that said 'Kitten Missing, Give Us A Call.' So it's gotta be deeper. And please, I beg you Sue, if you love me, don't ask me what."

"Who said that I loved you?"

"I've no idea." I grinned at her wickedly.

Sue did a glare.

"So then it's Sebastian," she said. "He picked up the kitten in Wigham and brought him to town."

"And why do you think so?"

"Well...we know he was up in Wigham and had a car, on account of that ticket you found in his pocket."

"Then how does O'Shaughnessy enter the plot?"

56

"Oh Sam, I don't *know*," she snapped. "I don't *know*. I mean anything's possible."

"Bingo," I said. "So you're wasting your time if you're making up stories. Besides, how he got here is only the start because now we've got mystery people like Patter and— Hold it a second!" I leapt to the phone. "You mind if I use this?"

"Why would I mind? It's not like I pay for it."

"Right. That's a point." I stepped on the speaker and punched out a call to the neighborhood precinct, a personal line. A fellow I know there, a cat named Gomez, is onto the trick of a personal phone. He uses a cell phone that's stashed in the closet where stuff from the criminals goes when they're caught and it works pretty nicely. The calls are private, they're uninterrupted, and criminals pay.

He answered it promptly. "Seventh Precinct, Officer Gomez."

"Buddy, it's Sam. Can you do me a favor?"

"I ever say no? How you doin there, Sammy?"

"Lousy," I said. "How's life at the precinct?"

"Busy," he said. "They keep opening the closet and stashin' more stuff. Like I can't get a nap in. You better talk fast."

"Can you do me a search on a Peter Patter?"

"Sounds like an alias."

"Looks like a creep. Call him a burglar who works with a dart gun. Blond about thirty."

"Consider it done. I'll get on the computer when Rafferty's off and get back to you, Sammy."

I hung up the phone. "Okay where was I?"

"The mystery people. You don't know a thing about Mittens and G."

"Did I actually say that?"

"No, but you thought it.—C'mere for a back rub."

I jumped at the chance. I moved to the pillow and Sue started carefully, merrily dancing around on my spine. "Boy you are tense," she said. "Try relaxing."

I tried relaxing.

"Continue," she said.

I continued relaxing, and started to yawn.

"Hey, I meant talking. Continue talking."

"Mmmmm..." I said, yawning, and tumbled to sleep.

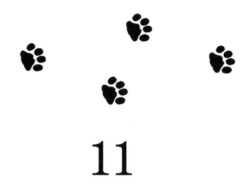

11

I woke, fuzzy, at 10:30. It took me a second to know where I was and a couple of seconds to know *when* I was: Sunday morning. Good. That was fine. Kitten Kaboodle is closed for the day and Hunnicker's shop doesn't open till noon. I had to hurry but not to scram.

I stretched slowly and leapt to the floor. Sue was asleep on the edge of a pillow. I nuzzled her shoulder and cat-footed out and went back to the office.

Nobody home. No lying brunettes, no cheap Continentals, no five pound lobsters, not even a mouse. The plastic pistol was still on the desk and I carted it quickly to one of the shelves where it dribbled some ammo, but not very much. I checked the machine. There was nothing on it. I looked at the food bowl where Hunnicker'd left me the usual breakfast of dubious crud and a tepid bowlful of yesterday's water. I drank some water and went to the desk where the Mac was flashing. I opened the mail.

The first was from Buster: Patter'd checked out.
I groaned at the blotter and pounded the "Next."

FROM: Rafferty-JQ@7thPrecinct.com
DATE: Sunday, December 12, 4:27 AM (EST)
TO: sam@samthecat.com
SUBJECT: PATTER

Hi, Sammy. Here's what I got. "Peter Patter"
is Herman Hench. Wanted by Interpol. Known
to trade in endangered species. Never been
caught. Known to be armed with a dangerous
dart gun. Careful, amigo. Yrs, Gomez.

I stared at it stupidly. *What did it mean?*

I was mulling it over when *whirr, clank,* I heard
the old rumbling sound in the wall: the dumbwaiter
coming. I knew it was Spike and the door slid open
and Spike jetted out and then landed precisely on top
of the Mac.

"Have you rescued the kitten?" he started, "and
solved the unsolvable mysteries and gotten the girl?"

I shot him a look full of bullets and daggers.

"Oof! Ya got me!" He fell to the floor and then,
writhing in agony, suddenly died.

"When I need a comic..." I said.

"C'mon. I was actually serious, Sam." He got up
and came back to the blotter. "I thought you'd be
done."

"Then go back to the carpet," I said to him tightly.
"I think I liked you a lot better dead. You were more
realistic."

"It's not going well."

"It's not even going." I stared at the wall.

He was reading the e-message over my shoulder.

"Endangered species?" he said.

"I know."

"Are Malteses endangered?"

"This one is."

I exited e-mail and pounced on the key that provided the key to the world wide web. *Beaumont Nursery*, I typed under *Search*. A second later it crowded my screen with a menu of Beaumonts. I took #3— *The Beaumont Nursery at Beaumont Farms*. I got to a website showing a shot of a pleasant cottage surrounded by trees, and right underneath it, a shot of the guy in Sebastian's wallet— the pleasant old man who was smiling like Santa and holding a cat. On the cottage behind him, I spotted the sign that said *Beaumont Nursery, Wigham, New York*.

In 1960, the copy read, *Algernon Beaumont (shown here) created the Nursery at Beaumont Farms with a family of kittens imported from France. For half a century, these charming Malteses have taken prizes and captured hearts. For how to adopt one, inquire* HERE.

I clicked on the *HERE* where I learned that a kitten could now be adopted for 800 bucks

So could that be the answer? 800 bucks? In the 21st Century, 800 bucks wasn't much of a fortune. Hardly enough to entice any game-hunters into the game. And hardly enough to pay three week's rent on a Village apartment.

Spike shook his head. "So how about this?" he said, looking creative. "The kid swallowed diamonds. They're still in his gut and the thieves are all after him. What do you think? Or how about this one? The kitten's a clone. Or an alien being—"

61

"The Kitten from Mars?"

"—and these scientists want him for—"

"Spike," I said. "Stop! Do you want to be help-ful?"

He nodded. "Of course. And Donna went out, by the way, so I'm free."

"Then go up to Kaboodle and hang out with Brigid and—"

Spike shook his head at me. "Already gone."

"Gone?" I said stupidly.

"Gone with the dawn. I was up on my windowsill, watching the street? and I happened to see her. She told me to tell you she had to go home or O'Shaughnessy'd yowl, but she'd talk to you later. She didn't say when."

I thought for a second and flicked at the screen. "Then work the computer," I said. "You could start with a search on Patter— I mean on Hench— and then see what you get on endangered species."

"You think that's important?"

I said, "I don't know."

He nodded agreeably. "What about you? You want to confide what your secretive plans are?"

I leapt to the window and scowled at him, "No."

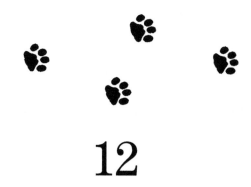

12

My secretive plans came in three different parts. The first and most pressing was finding a witness to last night's adventure in back of the Pearl. If somebody'd clobbered our Mr. Mittens and taken the kitten, I had to know who, since the fate of the kitten—his health and safety— was vital and urgent, and everything else was just twists in a mystery, ploys in a plot.

It wasn't bad out. In fact, it was warmer. The sun was shining, the wind had been tamed, and most of the snow had been salted and plowed so the streets weren't skating rinks. Islands of slush were collected at curbsides but easy to leap and the walk to the alley was pleasantly bracing.

I got there quickly and eyeballed the scene. Nobody'd bothered to plow in the alley and giant footsteps were punched in the snow from the spot where the body had lain with the bag. Nothing remained but the giant footsteps that ended abruptly in general slush.

I looked up at the windows that looked at the alley. I noted some life behind one of the drapes and I followed its lead to a building on Bedford. The house in question was three stories high and had casement windows and vine-covered walls and a fine-looking stoop that led up to an entry that posted a plaque at the side of its door: *Dr. Abraham Shrank*, it announced to the reader, *Therapy, Counseling, Ego Massage.*

I leapt from the stoop to the ledge of a window that didn't have curtains, and peered at a room. The room was as clean as a G-rated movie. A polished floor and a leather-like chaise and a bentwood rocker; that, and a lamp that looked like a mushroom deported from Mars. A middle-aged tabby, arranged on the rocker, appeared to be sleeping. I knocked at the pane. She looked up at me idly and came to the sill.

"Do you have an appointment?" she mouthed through the window.

I had to say yes or I'd never get in so I nodded politely. She reached for the catch and then pushed the thing open. I leapt to the floor.

"And your name?" she said.

"Sam."

"And you say you're expected?"

I shook my head slowly. "I'm not," I said. "No. I misrepresented. But, ma'am, it's a matter of—"

"Ah! Life and death?"

"I'm afraid so."

"Of course." She moved back to her rocker and flicked at the chaise. "Have a seat," she said nicely, and watched as I sat, her alert little eyes unrelentingly cheerful, her manner efficient and distantly warm. "Well, you're truly in luck," she said, after I'd settled. "Our twelve o'clock canceled because of the snow. So how can I help you?"

"It's more than just me. It's a kidnapped kitten," I said, plunging in. "He was nabbed last night in your next-door alley. I thought if you'd seen it you might fill me in."

"I assume you're his father?"

I shook my head no. "I'm a private detective."

"Ah ha. I see." She looked up at me thoughtfully. "Yes indeed. I once had a patient—" she rocked in her chair— "who completely believed she was Sherlock Holmes. But once we examined the obvious difference—that *he*, of course, was a British shorthair, and *she*, of course, was a Scottish Fold — well, we straightened it out in a matter of weeks."

"Forgive me, Madam, but—"

"Call me Doctor. I'm Dr. Laura," she said. "That's my name."

"You're an actual doctor?"

"Of course I'm a doctor. I share the office with Dr. Shrank. I work with the children. I settle them down. I work with the seniors. I liven them up. And then on the weekends I manage the Saturday evening Twelve Paw therapy group."

"Twelve...Paw?"

"Three cats. We get together and talk about Issues."

I said, "Issues."

She said, "You know. Anger management..? catnip addiction..? eating disorders? The usual stuff." She regarded me closely and rocked in her chair. "Do

I sense that you're angry?"

I said, "Not me."

"A little impatient?"

"Perhaps impatient to get to your answer. The kitten is—"

"Ah! Impatience is anger, you know. In disguise. I'd really suggest that you come to the group. We could tackle your anger and then, while we're up, we could deal with that Sherlock delusion too."

"Could we tackle the kitten?" I said. "Did you actually happen to see him?"

"In fact, I did. It was just around midnight, and passingly strange. A gigantic redhead appeared in the alley and walked by the building—the Salsbury house? where they're putting the roof up? And suddenly, bam! This complete piece of lumber just *blew* off the roof and knocked him unconscious."

"So *that's* it," I said. I pictured the lumber I'd seen on the roof, and the wind that had blown like a dinosaur's sneeze. I could see how it happened. I figured the evidence must've been buried in some of that snow. "But then where was the kitten—"

"The kitten ran off. He jumped out of some luggage and ran to the left."

I sighed and looked broken. "That means that he's lost."

"But he isn't," she chirped. "He ran off to the left. To that bend in the alley? You know, by the Pearl? And another man found him and gathered him up. He was holding a carrier. Isn't that nice? He just happened to have it."

"Just happened," I said. "Did you see what he looked like?"

"Oh yes. He was quite handsome. What I saw of him most was the top of his head. He had nice dark hair with a big streak of white."

"Did you see where he went to?"

"I didn't," she said. "But what does it matter? The kitten is safe and the ending is happy. The problem," she said, "is that *you* aren't happy. Perhaps it's your guilt. Or a troublesome youth that's entrapped your emotions and frozen your heart and deprived you of joy."

"Uh-huh. Perhaps," I said, rapidly rising. "Thanks, Dr. Laura. You've been quite a help."

"So we'll see you next Saturday? 12:45?"

I turned at the window and squinted. "You will?"

"To discuss your emotions. Your strangled intentions. Your lack of commitment."

I leapt to the street.

At the corner of Bedford, a voice from somewhere yelled, "'Scuse me, darlin!" I followed the voice to a parked Mercedes with Florida plates, and then lifted my eyes to the half-open window. A trio of knockouts were posed at the pane and the odor of woman was flooding the street like the odor of fish spilling out of a can. They were white Angoras, blue-eyed and slim, with those pink little noses and pink little ears.

"Are you talking to me?" I said, half-distracted, but not so distracted I didn't leap up like a fur-coated yo-yo.

They nodded their heads.

"Can you tell us the time?" said the one in the

center.

"It's just around noon," I said. "Something like that."

"Is there somethin to do here," she drawled, "around noon? We've got hours to kill till the driver gets back and we're goin bananas. We'd like somethin safe but completely New Yorky— you know what ah mean?"

I suddenly thought about Madam LaZonga. Three little princesses. One dozen paws. You'll meet them on Sunday, she'd said, around noon. I owed her a kindness. I pay what I owe.

"The Gypsy Tearoom," I said. "It's safe, and about as New Yorky as anything gets."

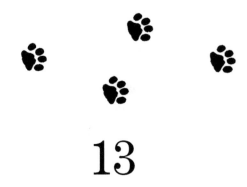

13

The neon sign at The Fatal Fedora was shimmering brightly and doing its thing. *"Tricks can be treats,"* it was blinking in yellow and burbling in purple, *"It's fun to be fooled."*

Oh no it isn't, I thought. I'd been tricked and treated to garbage since Saturday night. I'd been trapped in a Fun House where meaningless villains popped up in the hallways and stuck out their tongues and then popped back down again, laughing like loons. There had to be sense in it somewhere, I thought, and maybe the trick was to start the thing over— go back to the get-go and see what I got. The questions were obvious:

Who was the kitten? who was he really? and why was he hot?

The Beaumont Gallery was just as I left it. The smashed-open window was still just as smashed, and

I found Jean-Clawed on the office desk chair, looking as perfectly groomed as before. He was snacking on Kibble.

"Welcome, Monsieur," he said, wiping his whiskers. "A pleasure indeed."

"I came to talk business," I said. "We alone?"

He nodded agreement and gestured me in to a seat on the table. Sebastian's luggage, I noted with interest, was gone from the floor. "Monsieur Sebastian," he added, "is gone. He left with his brother."

"His brother?"

"Jacques. The gallery's owner. They left about nine."

"Without the kitten?"

"Without a doubt." He pawed at his whiskers again. "You tell me you come to talk business. But tell me, Monsieur. Are you here for Miss Brigid?"

"I can't really say."

"You mean you don't want to."

"I mean I don't know."

"Then your mind is still open?"

"Let's say that it's empty. Let's say that it's screaming to get itself filled. I need information before I can hack it for either one of you. Start with the kid, and with what makes him special."

"I hope you've got time. It's a very long story," he murmured.

"Then start."

"Would you care for some catnip?"

I shook my head no.

"That's a pity, Monsieur. It's an excellent blend." He looked down at his Kibble and took the last bite.

"This tale will amaze you, Monsieur, and I say that knowing detectives are rarely amazed. A man of your background— a man of the world— has heard dozens of stories, but this one is true which is why it's amazing."

I nodded. "Go on."

"And what, may I ask, do you know about Malta?"

"I know it's an island. Somewhere near Italy."

"Bravo, Monsieur. You are smarter than most. My story begins on the island of Malta in 1520."

I looked at the clock. "Could we start a bit later?"

He shook his head no.

I looked up at him quickly but buttoned my lip.

"My family line is descended from Malta. The island itself had been conquered by Spain but the king had returned it on one condition. That every year on the Fourth of July the people of Malta would send him a pair of their Maltese kittens. A boy and a girl."

"He gave up an island for two little kittens?"

"They gave up the kittens for too little land! The kittens had value, Monsieur. They were known for their beauty and talent. The island had what? A couple of palm trees and pieces of sand?" He was growing indignant.

I said, "You've a point. Please go on with your story."

He straightened his bow and leaned back on the cushion. "The annual shipment of 1580," he said, "went astray. It was put on the ship but through wicked fortune and evil intentions, it never arrived. The ship was attacked by a vicious pirate. He captured the galley and murdered the crew, but his

71

destiny fought him, Monsieur. A storm like a raging tiger came up from the sea and he couldn't defeat it. The ship went down. Down, down, Monsieur, to the depths. But as destiny had it—"

"—the kittens survived?"

"They floated to shore, Monsieur, on the back of a bottle of bourbon and landed in France. This is fact, Monsieur. You can look it up. It's in Kendleman's History of—"

"Skip it. Go on."

"Now about that catnip," he said, "are you sure?"

I nodded my certainty. "Still—help yourself."

I watched as he sniffed from a calico bag and then straightened his bow again. "Little is known," he continued contentedly, arching his spine, "little is known of the family's fortunes for many years until 1806 when two of its members arrived at the court of the Empress Josephine.—May I assume that you've heard of the Empress?"

"Napoleon's wife."

"But exactly, Monsieur. There's a famous portrait of Mimi La Belle on the Empress's lap. Perhaps you have seen it. It hangs in the Louvre."

I said, "Don't be silly."

He said, "Very well. Getting back to Napoleon—"

"Hold it," I said. "Can we cut to the present? I get the idea that your family is ancient—"

"And royal, Monsieur. We have royal blood in us. Contact with kings has invaded our blood and affected our genes."

"And Fluffer, the kitten?"

"His name is Louey."

"And what makes him special?"

72

"The kitten is gold."

"I beg your pardon?"

He pawed through a folder and slid me a photo across the desk, an eight-by-eleven, a glazed still.

It was a kitten. A kitten to make a robber kick a hole in a jeweler's window. Louey was golden, all right. The garishly gaudy gold of a sequin dress. His infant expression was much too mushy to give an impression of what he was like; he was still so tiny his eyes were closed. The caption beneath it said, *Born Yesterday: Golden kitten named Louis D'or. September 30 at Beaumont Farms.*

I narrowed my eyes and then looked at him sideways. "Publicity gimmick," I snarled. "It's a stunt."

"It's a stunt of nature, Monsieur. The kitten is not made of metal, of course, he is fur, but it's fur with a glitter. It's fur with a shine. He is totally special, Monsieur. And he's worth about two million dollars."

I lifted my ears.

He grinned at me briefly and sniffed some more herb.

"I see," I said carefully, not really seeing and not quite believing, but taking it in. "So how does Sebastian fit into the plot?"

"I have no idea, Monsieur. None at all. I wasn't aware he was back in the city till—what did you call him?—this...Patter arrived."

"You said *back* in the city."

"He lives in Wigham. In fact, Monsieur, he lives at the farm. He'd come for a visit and stayed for a week and then left to go home again."

"When did he leave?"

73

"It was right after dinner, Monsieur. I would say about 7:30 on Friday night."

"And he'd taken his luggage?"

"Indeed, Monsieur."

I thought for a moment. "All right, start again. So the next time you saw him—"

"Was Saturday night when he lay on the carpet, Monsieur. As I've said. I woke to the clatter of Mr. Patter, who shot at Sebastian—"

"And then?"

"I left. I must have returned around two in the morning, and there was Sebastian, Monsieur, on the phone. He was saying to Algernon, 'Pops, I found Louey but somebody dyed him,' and then he said, 'No. Will you listen, Papa? They stole him *again*,' and then Algernon's voice started screaming like thunder, 'You stupid idiot! Get yourself home!' But forgive me, Monsieur, he had screamed it in French so it sounded more elegant."

"That's the whole thing?"

"That's all that I know of. And right after that I went straight to your office."

I gave it some thought. The whole thing was goofy, but then life itself is occasionally goofy, so how can you tell? I needed some back-up. I needed some air. I rose from the table.

"There's two other things. A good-looking human with hair like a skunk.—Have you ever seen him?"

He shook his head no.

"Can you tell me who G is?"

"*Who?*" he said.

"G. You know. In my office. When Brigid was saying the kid in the treetop was someone from G."

"I paid no attention, Monsieur. The woman is clearly a liar and maybe a thief.— Which brings us full circle. For whom do you work? This redheaded liar," he offered, "or me?"

I looked at him squarely and said: "I don't know."

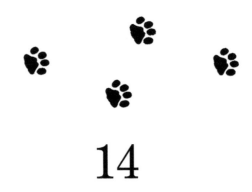

14

Istopped and had breakfast at Gus O'Malley's, a little Irish joint on the park. Gus is a sucker for any puss with a hustler's smile and a sorry tail and there's always a mixture of sharp-eyed locals and lucked-out grifters around on his floor. You want the street-talk, you go to Gus's, you gather an earful. The food isn't bad.

I worked my way in through the narrow alley and into a kitchen with clanging pots and the heady aroma of Irish bacon. Gus looked me over. "Hey, Sammy!" he yelled. "Long time, no seeya. C'mon. Have a seat."

I went off to a spot near the sink in the corner. 12:45 and the corner was jammed. Heavyweight mousers, exchanging whoppers; little old ladies with pavement-sore paws; and the girls from the alley, as skinny as dimes, with their fraying collars and ratty coats and those wrenchingly desperate kittenish smiles. I dodged their eyeballs and landed a spot next to Butch and Jane, who I know from the street.

"So how's it been goin?" I opened.

"Nah. It's been goin nasty. I'm lookin for work." Butch cocked his head at me, licking some wonderfully syrupy pancake crumbs from his nose. "Like I'd got me this gig down at Kammerman's Market. Night mouser. Sensational job. Fabulous set-up— perfect hours, great location, all I can eat. So what happens? They pass a law. No more cats allowed in a market. Last Friday? I'm outta work."

"He's becoming Republican," Jane butted in. "He wants the government off his back."

"And the special interests," Butch said to Jane. "I think I got clobbered by special interests."

"*What* special interests?" she argued.

Butch looked up at her crossly and snarled, "The mice!"

I didn't butt into it. Only a fool has political arguments. Nobody wins and it ruins your friendship as well as your meal. And this was a meal that I didn't want ruined. Gus had come up with a sizzling platter of crumbled bacon and scrambled eggs, the eggs scrambled softly and made with milk. The warm aroma was like a poem— a sensual sonnet, a radiant rhyme. An excellent breakfast, I've always figured, is fuel for the body but food for the soul.

I was licking my whiskers when Slasher came in. He did not come softly. He didn't have to. He walked like a man who's got several inches and ten pounds up on the rest of the world and the world better like it or lick a few lumps.

I looked up at Butch and said, "Kid, give me cover. I want to get out of here, quiet and fast."

Butch nodded quickly and covered my flanks as I raced to the exit.

"So what's got you ticked?" he said, out in the alley.

"The red Himalayan."

"You scared of him, Sammy?"

"Nope. Not at all. I just want to tail him as soon as he leaves and I don't want him onto me."

"Want any help?"

I said, "No, I don't think so, but thanks for the thought."

"Then I'll finish my breakfast," he said, backing off. "And I'll give him the eye he don't go on the lam."

I hid in a carton. Me and the corpse of an outcast geranium still in its pot and an empty can of DelMonte peaches. I waited patiently, low to the ground, in that hunter's position and stared at the door.

Nothing happened.

Twenty-five minutes of Nothing Happened and then Something Did.

He came wandering mindlessly out of O'Malley's, mellowed by breakfast and licking his paws. He didn't appear to expect to be followed. He took no precautions. He didn't look back. He started moving. I waited some more and then followed him silently, ten feet behind.

At the corner of Bleecker, he stopped for a light and I stopped at a kiosk, pretending to browse at the afternoon papers. Then I got snagged.

MISSING KITTEN VALUED
AT MILLIONS
Reward Posted at 50 K

I couldn't help it. I started to read.

WIGHAM, NY, Dec. 12—The story broke around 10 last night. The golden kitten—

I lifted my eyes and then raced to the corner. The Slasher was gone!

There was movement everywhere; color and light. The street was alive with the hustle of shoppers; tires hissed through the blackening slush, and a guy selling Christmas trees guarded his forest from three Pomeranians, ready to spritz, but the red Himalayan was nowhere in sight.

I peered past the legs of the booted tourists, the soggy sneakers, the muddy cuffs, the spattered-on bags from Banana Republic. And then I saw him.

Across Bleecker.

Sauntering jauntily into a shop with a faded awning: *The Healthier Pet.*

It all came together with one of those crashes that knocked all the crockery out of my head. Healthier Pet! The revolting cat food that lured little Fluffer from Patter's embrace. Or that lured little Louey from Hench's embrace. The number of changes in everyone's names was beginning to frazzle me; that part aside, I was feeling terrific. Little Jack Horner who'd stood on the corner and pulled out the plum.

I crossed at my leisure, taking my time about checking the windows in front of the store. Past the bags full of "Seaweed-enriched rice cakes," organic litter and "Kitti-Kat Kelp," I could see the interior—aisle after aisle of the tasteless and hideous totems of health.

I could see no humans and no other cats, not even the Slasher. I looked at the street. Then I looked at the cat door he must have gone in by. I took my chances and crashed through the slot.

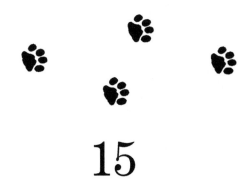

15

It was deathly quiet inside, and dim—the gloomy effect of organic lighting and kelp-enriched silence. I sniffed at the air. I detected the Slasher but didn't see him. And then I saw him. On top of a shelf, at the top of a carton marked *Vital Vittles, The Veggie Version of Virtual Veal.* For a terrible moment we locked eyes. And then he was on me, a million pounds of him scribbling tic-tac-toe on my spine while he hissed in my earlobe, "Get offa the case!"

I bucked like a bronco, which got me zilch. I decided to roll with it, rolling over and taking him with me. We rolled on the floor, rolling over and over, and over again, till we smacked on a barrel of *Mineral Mice, The Fortified Biscuit with Iron and— BAM!* The barrel went over and tipped on its side, emitting a mountain of Mineral Mice and a pouring of pellets that heaped on our heads. There must have been tons of them, raining down like a tropical deluge, a thundering storm that engulfed the horizon and roared in my ears.

For a frightening second I thought I was dead. I was looking at blackness, as black as a tomb. I was totally buried in vegetable rodents that smelled like turnips infected with beets, and I thought if it's over, I must be in Hell. Then I thought, if I'm thinking, I must be alive. I gathered some strength and I fought my way out of it, scrambling upward and into the air. Behind and below me, and under the mountain that seemed to be easily seven feet high, I could hear my opponent beginning his climb.

I leapt to the counter and braced for the fight. And then suddenly, *crack*, from behind an archway, a door popped open. A man came out, still wiping his hands on a paper towel. He looked at the mountain and, very suddenly, quite unexpectedly, started to laugh. I looked at him laughing, and started to gasp. *It was Mr. Mittens, the redheaded giant I'd seen in the alley.* I stayed very still. He hadn't seen me. I held my breath.

He moved to the mountain as Slasher surfaced. Slasher looked up at him. Slasher looked scared. Then a funny thing happened. The man, still laughing, went over and lifted the thug in the air, and said, "Slasher, Slasher. What've you done?" But he kept on laughing and settled the gangster on top of his shoulder and nuzzled his cheek.

Slasher looked goofy—as much in love as a teenage human, a moonstruck girl. I watched as the linebacker righted the barrel. He settled the Slasher on top of a box and said, "Listen. Stay there. I'm getting a broom," and then walked through the arch again.

Slasher turned. I moved down the counter and placed myself squarely in front of a rack full of porcelain plates. If he wanted to jump me, he'd shatter the plates, but he wouldn't want to; his friend would be mad.

He measured the distance and measured the cost. Then he shot me a look full of savage venom. "All right. So you got me now, pally," he rasped, "only now's not forever. You hurt my Jimmy, there ain't enough room in this city to hide."

I jerked at the archway. "Is that Mr. G?"

"Are you stupid on purpose?" he said, "or did somebody beat on your head with the side of a wall? Mr. G's just a customer. That there's Jimmy and Jimmy's my buddy and Jimmy's a saint. And I'm warnin ya, pally—"

I lifted my paw. "Look, I'm not after Jimmy—" I hoped I was right— "all I'm after's the kitten."

"The one at the Pearl?"

I nodded and waited.

"You won't hurt Jimmy?"

"I won't hurt Jimmy."

He glowered and glared. "My buddy Jimmy, he rescued my tail. I was out in a death row cell in Canarsie. The Peterson Pound, if ya heard of the joint. And I ain't done nothin. They never charged me or give me a lawyer or nothin like that. They was just gonna off me. And then came Jimmy. I'd lay down my life for him, honest to Pete."

I looked at him levelly. "Listen, Slasher, supposing my target was Mr. G. Do you think you could help me?"

"It might be arranged. He threatened my Jimmy."

I nodded. "Go on."

"So it's late last night," he said, "ten of eleven— we're open till midnight— this G comes in. So Jimmy looks up and says 'Hey! Mr. G!' like he already knows him, you know what I mean, only G ain't a smiler, ya know what I'm sayin? He leans on the counter and lays on a tale about some kinda burglar that's burgled a kitten to feed to his cobra and lammed to the Pearl. To Room Thirty-seven, he says. And then he pulls two hundred bucks from the seat of his pants and he says to my Jimmy, You rescue kittens? Go rescue me this one and come to my house."

"And Jimmy agrees to it?"

"Sure he agrees. I mean, second of all, he got use for the money, and mostly of all, he's a stand-up guy. And you're robbin' a robber, it ain't like a crime."

"So then what happened?"

"So Jimmy comes back about three in the morning with ice on his head and he phones Mr. G and he mumbles, I blew it. So then Mr. G has a fit on the phone. Like he threatens my Jimmy. He says he could fix it that Jimmy gets homeless and loses his store."

I thought for a moment. "So who's Mr. G?"

"I got no idea, pally. Nothin at all. I could say what he looks like. Whiter'n tuna and fatter'n turkey on Thanksgiving eve."

"I've got one other question," I said.

"You got *no* other questions, pally. You're done for the night." He gestured at Jimmy, who came through the archway. I leapt from the counter and raced to the door.

84

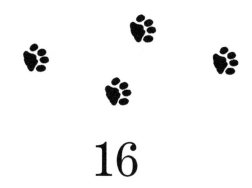

16

I entered the Pearl through the rear window and wandered around till I spotted Buster inspecting a Roach Motel in the hall. He looked up at me, grinning. "You want to see dumb? These guys are supposed to be older'n dirt, but you show em the corniest gag in the world and they always fall for it.— What's with the case?"

"I need a favor."

"Consider it done. Come on back to the office," he said, "and we'll shmooze. Like I figure the day-guy went up to the gym."

"You got a gym here?"

"We got a coupla heavyweight dumbbells in Room Twenty-eight. They been playin poker since Saturday night."

"Good luck to the day guy," I said. The office was small and crummy: a gray metal desk with an ancient computer, some dusty files, and a half-eaten roll on the afternoon's *Post.* The single chair, done in cracked plastic with nasty stuffing as gray as the desk, had been angled outward, as though the sitter had stared out the window and gnawed at his roll and looked out at his life passing by in a hurry and left in a hurry to try to catch up.

"So you keep any telephone records?" I asked him. "You know, like the calls that're made from the rooms?"

"Like from Room Thirty-seven?" He nodded. "Gotcha. Intelligent thinking."

He leapt to the desk and attacked the computer. I sat on the blotter and licked off some butter and glanced at the *Post*.

MISSING KITTEN VALUED AT MILLIONS
Reward Posted at 50 K

WIGHAM, NY, Dec. 12—The story broke around 10 last night. The golden kitten, named Louis D'Or, the first and only cat of his kind, was reported missing from Beaumont Farms.

Algernon Beaumont reported the crime, revealing the kitten had disappeared—between 9 PM Friday and just before dawn—from the Beaumont Nursery, right down the road from the Beaumont residence.

Tracks from the tires of several vehicles rutted the road, which led to the notion of foul play. The hefty reward—

"Okay, I got it!" Buster looked up at me, tapping the screen. I looked over his shoulder. "Saturday evening at 9:57," he said, "there's a call. It's a local number. And figure he made it at almost the instant he got to the room."

And before any news of the kidnapping broke and before he'd have known about any reward. And he'd called it again at the top of the morning. I stared at the number.

"Is that any help?"

"It might be later," I said. "If I'm right."

"Okay—what's the story?"

I pounded my tail on the open newspaper. "*That* is," I said.

Buster looked down at it. "Man, you're kidding! I saw it last night on the ten o'clock news. But it didn't occur to me—"

"Well, why would it? That was the point about dying him black. A gold-plated kitten would catch a few eyes and the gig would be over."

"What else have you got to amaze and astound me?"

I told him the rest. That Peter Patter was Herman Hench with a record for poaching endangered species. That Slasher's Jimmy—our Mr. Mittens—had somehow or other been hired by G.

"Only hold it a second. Not that I doubt you, but how would this G know where Louey *was*? "

I looked up at the number on Buster's screen. "A ten gets you twenty, it gets me to G."

For a time he was silent, his blue eyes thoughtful, his brown face somber, his tail in a knot as he tapped with it rhythmically, beating the desk. "So you're telling me G knew where Louey was because Hench must've called him?"

"That's what I'd guess."

"Only why would he call him? Wait. Don't tell me." Again he was silent. He angled his head. "Because maybe he'd kidnapped the kitten for G? Or like, G was his customer?"

"That's what I'd guess."

"But if G hired Hench, and if Hench had the kitten, then why hire Jimmy to steal him from Hench?"

"That's a logical question." I said, "and I don't have a logical answer."

"Like maybe you're wrong?"

"That's a logical answer." I lowered my head.

"Look, I hate to do downers—"

I said, "While you're down, let me tell you the rest of it."

"Oy," he said.

"Right." I reported the story from Dr. Laura.

He thought it over and scratched at his chin. "Mysterious Stranger with stripes in his hair?" He looked up at me darkly. "Then everything else is completely irrelevant, isn't it, Sam? I mean G and Jimmy and everyone else?"

"But I'm figuring otherwise."

"Figuring how?"

I wriggled uncomfortably. "Figuring—look—it's like everything spins around Mr. G. Like the web to the spider, you know what I'm saying? Like G'd be the spider and everyone else in this cockeyed concoction is part of his web."

"Like including the Stranger?"

I nodded. "Yeah. But I don't know the answer."

I started to rise. "I'll go back to the office and play with the phone."

"Let me give you my number," he said. "What you do is, you phone up the switchboard and press two-oh."

"And that's where I'll find you? In Room Twenty?"

He nodded briefly. "That's where I'll be. Or at least till tomorrow. The only ones in there are me and the silverfish. Man, they are fast. They race in the bathtub, you know? Got a couple of friends that come over, we bet on the race. You're welcome to stay but I—"

"Yeah. Gotta go." I rose from the paper. "I'll give you a call, let you in on the upshot."

"You'd better," he said.

I decided to leave by the lobby exit. The lobby was empty except for the dust that was floating like moonbeams on yesterday's air. When I got to the palm tree, I noticed the Rex, the improbable Wilmer, arranged on a couch and entirely lost in the depths of the *Times*. The gigantic paper, completely open, sat like a tent on the top of his head and his eyes peered out of it, casing the room.

I crossed the lobby and sat down beside him and said, without color, "So how's Mr. G?"

The Rex ignored me, pretending to read.

I glanced at a palm tree and said, "Where is he?"

His eyes crawled sideways. He muttered, "Who?"

"You heard me the first time," I said, "Mr. G."

He spat at me, "Beat it."

I growled in my throat. "You got his number?"

I said. "He gave me a message to call him."

"So why'd he do *that*?"

"I don't know till I call him," I said. "But maybe he misses your company. How about that? Like he wants me to find you."

The Rex made a snort. His pale little face seemed to twist in a smile that had cynical knowledge that clashed with his youth. "Oh yeah, he misses me. Yeah, that's a fact. The last time I seen him, he shoots me with water and shows me his boot-heel and tosses me out."

"I suppose you were trespassing."

"Yeah? What's that?"

"That you'd entered illegally."

"Yeah? Well, you're wrong. I been livin there legally, right from the start. And then I just *once*—like on Saturday morning—I happened to chuck on his idiot rug—his exciting Siberian tiger rug—and it's outta the window and never come back."

"Siberian tiger?"

"That's what he said. But you want my opinion, it looks like nothin that looks like a tiger. It don't got teeth and it smells like cinnamon."

"Cinnamon, eh? Well supposing I call him. And just supposing he tells me to find you. So what should I say?"

"You can tell him forget it. You tell him I hope he has fun with his tiger. You tell him I'm through."

I rose from the sofa. "So what's his number?"

The Rex sped it off to me.

"Bingo!" I said. It was, as I'd figured, the local number that Hench had called twice from the phone in his room. "So what's his address?" I began, when

Buster came out of the office and glanced at the couch. He trotted on over. "He givin you trouble?" He jerked at Wilmer.

I said, "I don't know." I looked back at Wilmer, still under the *Times*. "Are you giving me trouble, or G's address?"

Buster stood over him, looking large and yet not unfriendly. Wilmer looked out. "If I say the address," he said, squinting at Buster, "you let me stay here as long as I want?"

Buster looked doubtful. He groaned in his throat and then looked back at Wilmer. "You got no home?"

"Man, I got no *life* if I rat on the fatso."

Buster looked gloomy, but nodded twice. "You'll have to be careful and do what I tell you..."

"I'll do what you tell me."

He nodded. "Fine. Then tell me this character's name and address."

"It's Caspar Gutless," Wilmer said swiftly. "He lives on Twelfth Street. Two-twenty-one."

17

The Gutless mansion was even large by the standard of mansions— two houses wide and three stories high with a dormered roof and a private garden that played at the rear. Wilmer had said there'd be open windows. "Almost everywhere," Wilmer had said. Apparently Gutless indulged in a single nightly after-dinner cigar— an expensive Havana that smelled pretty nifty and passingly mellow, or so Wilmer'd said— but the Gutless butler, a Brit named Kent, liked to open the windows as wide as he could, and in every weather, at every chance, afraid of the odor but not of the drafts which had murdered the house plants, the tropical fish and, according to Wilmer, the two Gutless wives.

One man's mead is another's poison. The open windows—I counted seven gigantic casements— were joy to our hearts.

"Which one do you want?" Buster said as we stood there. Buster'd insisted on coming along and

I didn't object to it. Buster himself had a nice steady manner, a confident way that inspired my confidence.

"None of them yet." I examined the garden—its soggy bushes and scraggly ivy and bare-headed trees, one of which climbed towards an open window. I jerked at the window. "That one," I said.

Buster looked dubious. "Second story?"

"A likelier place to have private rooms."

"Like the kind of a room where you might keep a kitten?"

"Or anything else meant for private eyes."

He shrugged and then followed me. Up to the branches, out on a limb, and then into the house.

The very rich, someone famously offered, are very different from you and me and the room that we entered was very different. The first impression was total gloom. The walls were dark and mahogany-paneled, the several windows had wine-colored drapes. On the left-hand panel, a sputtering fire was alive in a fireplace, lighting the rug that was laid out in front of it, fleshless and flat as a crime-scene outline of somebody's corpse.

The rug was a tiger all right, or had been. Its glowing pelt had a pattern of stripes, and whoever had skinned it had very carefully kept it together and left it its head. Wilmer was right, though. It didn't have teeth. Its mouth was agape in a toothless snarl and its glittering eyes had an absence of soul.

We stood for a moment, stopped in our tracks at the awesome horror of what had been done. That such a creature, a big brother, had given his life to wind up as a rug seemed as sorry a story as ever got told, and we stood there in silence, in deep contemplation of life and its meaning or lack thereof.

"Of course...he'd've eaten us," Buster said softly. "I mean if he'd seen us."

I nodded. "I know." It's the part about nature I've never liked. That creatures were made to destroy other creatures. And man was a creature like everyone else. A born hunter. The only difference, it seemed, was that mankind would do it for rugs. But what kind of difference was that to the prey? It would not have appeased me, I figured, to know that I'd died for the greater nutrition of tigers or even to wind up as mulch for a plant, so why did the notion of subbing for nylon appear to be harsher and more of a waste?

I lifted my eyes as though looking for guidance, and that's when I saw what he had on the walls: Heads of animals, mostly cats. I spotted a leopard, a lynx, a jaguar, another tiger. I started to reel. An entire jungle was here in Manhattan. Endangered creatures who'd once had a life and a chance at a future were nailed to the wall and I felt revulsion and waves of pity. Pity for all of us, doomed by nature to live by the tooth, the claw and the gun, but the scene that surrounded me went beyond nature. That was the difference and that was the twist. Nature kills but she doesn't murder. And this was murder.

"It's not only cats," Buster said in a whisper. His blue eyes misted and circled the room. Over the mantel, suspended by chains, was the tusk of an elephant. Down on the floor was a tortoise foot stool with tortoise feet. And up on the couch was an antelope afghan the size of a blanket.

Buster said, "Geez! I mean what would you call this? A zoo of the dead?"

I nodded grimly. "I'd call it quits if it weren't for Louey. Come on. Let's go. Let's look for the kitten and try to get out."

"Should we look on the floor?" Buster said, "or the ceiling?"

"Don't even think it," I said. "Let's go."

We moved very softly, out to a hallway with woolen carpets and polished floors and a series of archways and half open doors.

"So how are we doing this?" Buster whispered. "You want to split up or you want to stay—"

"Ssh!"

We both went silent and angled our ears. From somewhere below us, the sound of footsteps: the squeak of wing-tips on carpeted stairs.

We raced down the hallway and into a room that looked perfectly normal. Sofas and chairs, none of them mammals, present or past, and some non-amphibian tables and stools. From behind a doorway within the room, came the whisper of breathing and odors of smoke. The squeaks pursued us. We dashed to the couch and then ducked underneath it, in back of its skirt, as the squeaky wing-tips came into the room.

Squeaks on the carpet.

Knocks on the door.

The voice behind it said, "*Now* what, Kent? You're aware that I'm working?" The voice was fat. It was partly rumble and partly purr— that fleshy sound that comes out of a throat that's been thor-

95

oughly buttered and clotted with cream. The voice in front of it dithered Britishly, "Mr. Hench has arrived, Mr. G."

"Mr. Hench is early by half an hour. Should I keep him waiting?" The clotted voice seemed to toy with the thought like a dog with a bone.

"Whatever you say, sir. Whatever you say."

"He could sit on the sofa and stare at his toes and get terribly angry."

"They usually do."

"And would that be amusing?"

"Indeed, Mr. G."

"It would *not* be amusing," the fat voice rumbled, "so open the door, man, and send him on in."

Clickety-creak as the door opened.

Squeak-squeak as the butler went out.

We lay very still in our silk-lined bunker, not even breathing or twitching our ears. Something was under me, poking my gut, and I squirmed to get rid of it, kicked it away. What it turned out to be was a leaky ballpoint. A dimestore pen in a millionaire's house. I thought it was funny. I didn't laugh. I kept not-laughing as Squeaky Wingtips returned to the hallway and said, "Go in."

I couldn't resist it. I poked my head out and netted a vision of tasseled loafers, designer khakis and Herman Hench, the blond Peter Patter I'd seen at The Pearl. I pulled my head in and winked at Buster.

Caspar Gutless said, "Well and well."

The door closed quietly.

Herman Hench said, "You wanted to see me." His voice was sharp with the spin of an accent; German,

I thought.

"When a man kills a tiger but loses a kitten, he has to be seen, sir, to be believed." The fat voice chuckled but wasn't amused. "I wanted to watch as you made your excuses."

"I ran into trouble," said Hench, "from the start."

"Trouble, indeed, sir. Trouble, indeed. I gave you complete and specific instructions. I drew you a map of the Beaumont farm. And you sat in that chair, sir, that very chair on Friday at tea time and said 'it's a deal.' And you took my money, sir, quite a good bit."

"And I've since learned the kitten's worth many times more."

"So you're holding out on me."

Sound of a lighter clicking a flame on. Buster looked up. We listened intently as Hench said: "Perhaps."

"Ah-hah! Very good, sir. Ha! Very good. When you called me this morning and said he was gone after saying last night that you had him in hand, I was mighty suspicious, sir. Mighty upset. So now what's the story? You have him or not?"

"Are you willing to equal the Beaumont's reward?"

"The fifty thousand?" The fat man laughed. "But upon delivery, sir. Make it tonight—"

"Better make it tomorrow. I'll need some more time."

"I see. Very well, sir. Then this is the deal. I'll see you on Monday at nine PM. You'll deliver the goods or return my deposit. I'll have your word on it."

"Yes. All right."

"And I'm certain you'll honor it. After all, we've been doing business for so many years. Now where can I reach you?"

"At—"

"Please write it down." A moment of silence. Then: "Ah, I see. If you're heading there now, you can buy me a taxi. I have an appointment."

The scraping of chairs.

The *click* and the *creak* as the door popped open.

I poked my head out, recording a glimpse of a man as obese as a man can be and still remain mobile. The view from the side was like watching the shape of the letter D with some feet at the bottom, an arm at the side, and a round O head like a mushy melon with whipped-cream ringlets of dead-white hair. Hench followed after him. Traveling slowly, they went through the doorway. I watched their retreat.

Sound of their footsteps, hushed by the carpet. And Caspar Gutless's bellowing, *"Kent! I shall need my overcoat."*

Then silence.

We waited, motionless.

After a time, Buster said quietly, "Let's hit the road."

And that's when I uttered the idiot words that were almost my last ones. "No," I said. "Wait. Cover my tail while I look in the office. I just want to see Mr. Hench's address."

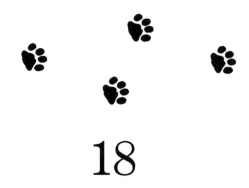

18

So there I was, minding Gutless's business, pawing through papers on top of his desk and exploring for something with Hench's address, when I spotted his lighter— a very elaborate silver cigar lighter, shaped like a cat, and engraved with the signature, *H.H.* The initials spelled trouble, and something rapid and cold and nasty was licking my spine like a hideous spider. It crawled to my ear and then started to scream at me, "Hurry and hide!" except it was Buster, hollering hoarsely from out in the hallway, "Sammy! It's Hench!"

I ducked for cover. I would have been fine. Except Buster wasn't. I heard the yowl; then I heard the growl; then I heard the "Oof!" and went rocketing out to the scene of the battle. The scene was ugly. The battle was pitched. Buster was biting at Hench's ankle. Hench, in his pea coat, was aiming a fist that would elevate Buster to Gutless's wall with a plaque and a mounting instead of a neck.

I leapt from the carpet and chipped at his hand. It wasn't enough but it got him distracted and Buster let go of him just as he whirled. Only now it was me he was suddenly after. I raced for the dooway. He started to chase. He was chased by Buster. I ran through an arch and wound up in a drawing room, lurid with birds in Victorian cages. They started to shriek. "There's somebody coming!" they hollered. "Quiet! There's somebody coming!" And somebody came. It was Herman Hench with his dart gun pointed. I leapt to a parrot cage, ducking a dart but disturbing a door which escaped on its spring as the parrot came out of it, swooping at Hench like an F-16 on a warrior's flight and beginning to peck at him. Buster arrived, took a look at the action and, catching its drift, sprung a couple of latches and freed some more birds. We raced to the hallway and started to run for a room with a window. We made a few yards but then Hench was pursuing us— Hench, with the parrots still pecking his shoulders and eating his ears, was intent on protecting them; killing a couple of neighborhood cats wouldn't get in his way. He lifted his pistol and whooshed out a dart. It narrowly missed me. We got to a room with a wide open door and a boat-sized bed and then raced underneath it and leapt to a sill that looked over on Twelfth Street and started to leap.

I felt the sting as the dart hit my shoulder and ricocheted off me. The cinnamon smell was ripe in my nostrils and clung to my pelt.

I remember landing. I hit the sidewalk with Buster beside me. And then I was out.

I remember dreaming. I dreamt of jungles. I dreamt of tigers on Russian plains, and exquisite tortoises, old as the world, whose incredible ancestors probably lived before cats were invented. I dreamt of birds, and I dreamt of Dumbo, who learned how to fly, and I dreamt of animals, two by two, and how Noah saved them and weathered the flood and I dreamt of Louey and dreamt of Hench, pursuing the lot of us, dart gun in hand, until nothing was left of us. No more cats and no other creatures but Gutless and Hench.

I woke in the alley where Buster'd dragged me. Buster was next to me. Buster said, "Hi." I mumbled, "What time is it?" Buster said, "Two-and-a-half hours later."

I managed an "Oh."

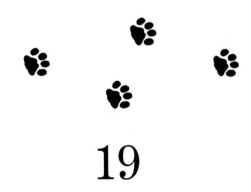

19

How can I describe this? I felt as though I was looking at the world through a thick pane of plate glass. Or watching a movie I wasn't in. I was physically there but I wasn't present. If someone yelled "Fire!" I'd've thought, "Uh-huh," but I wouldn't have stirred myself. Nothing was real or alive or important. Including me. So this was Drugs, I thought, slowly and vaguely. I didn't like them. It wasn't fun. I'd just say no on the next occasion when somebody offered to shoot me with darts.

I tried to get up but my legs didn't want to. Why would they want to? They weren't legs, they were rubber hoses. My mouth was dry. It wanted water. Perhaps the hose could provide them with water. I thought that was cute. I thought it was funny. I started to laugh. I lay in the alley and laughed like a nut. The laughter scared me. I wanted to sleep, but Buster insisted I try to get up. I thought I could do it. Cats have done more. Some, I've been told, have even made leaps as high as a footstool. I tried it again. This time I managed to stand on my paws. I was ready for anything now. The Olympics medal for Standing.

Buster said, "Walk."

It seemed like an interesting, funny idea. I started walking. Walking was nice. It was something like dancing, without the music. I started humming.

Buster said, "Man, you are just so out of it. Lucky I stayed."

"For which I thank you," I said, "from my bottom."

He looked at me sideways.

I said, "From my heart. From the heart of my bottom. Is that how it goes?"

He looked at me sharply. "I'm walking you home."

"Hey, you really don't have to."

"Of course I have to. You saved my life, Sam. You hadn't come in, he'd've killed me for certain.— Watch it," he said, "or you'll step in that puddle."

I saw the puddle and even leapt it. I said, "So there!"

We were almost at Bleecker. The street was dark and the air was colder, a wind coming in with a raw touch of moisture, a promise of snow. It was clearing my head though. I said, "What happened? I mean...how'd you happen to tangle with Hench?"

"Well I just wasn't certain you'd heard my warning. He crossed to the office—"

"To pick up his lighter—"

"—I barreled ahead and he stepped on my tail. And then I attacked him. I can't say for sure if I did it to help you or just out of rage."

103

"And speaking of rage," I said, "some of those parrots had personal grudges."

"It looked like it, huh? I mean basically parrots are peaceable birds."

I stopped at the bookstore. "You want to come in?"

"If you're really okay—" Buster looked at me closely— "I'd kind of prefer getting back to the Pearl."

"To the silverfish races," I added. "Sure."

"There's this sweet little filly," he said. "A two-year-old out of the drainpipe. I think she's got speed. 'Course it all depends if the bathtub's wet. But you know where to reach me," he said.

"Room Twenty."

He nodded slowly.

I wished him luck.

A Sony radio played on the pink linoleum counter at Kitten Kaboodle. Against the darkness, a sweet soprano sang about silent and holy and bright and Sue, with a ribbon as green as her eyes, lay directly on top of it, lit from below by the flattering glow of its luminous dial. I was standing beside her, enjoying some cream from a porcelain saucer. It wasn't my first.

"I believe you've recovered," she noted. "Except for requiring a bath and a nightful of sleep. If you like, you can stay here." She flicked her tail at the pink quilted sofa, and angled her head.

"Why, a fellow'd be crazy," I mumbled, "to leave."

"If the fellow in question," she muttered, "were actually sane to begin with. But you, you jerk, like

104

you'd rather go rattling around in some alley and get yourself shot at."

I lifted my eyes. "I didn't get shot," I announced, "in an alley."

"Of course not," she said. "You got shot in the butt."

"I got shot in a mansion."

"I'm *truly* impressed." She was rolling her eyes to make clear that she wasn't. "You're such a tough-guy," she said, "such a sap— you'll go back again Monday and get yourself killed."

"And why would I do that?" I'd finished my cream and was slapping that thirsty look back on my face.

She appeared to ignore it. "Because," she said sharply, "it all leads to Gutless. To Gutless and Hench. Hench has the kitten—he said so himself—and at nine o'clock Monday—"

"He's lying," I said. "Hench doesn't have him. He's stalling for time. Oh he might go hunting. He'll check in the alleys, he'll check in the gutters, he'll look in the pounds, but he doesn't have him. Hench is a blond. And whoever's got Louey has skunk-like hair. So it isn't that simple."

"Well how about this?" She stood up on the radio, scratching her nails on the top of the grillwork and arching her spine. "How's about whatshername— Doctor Laura— how's about maybe she might've been wrong? How's about maybe she looked out the window and saw Hench's watch cap and thought it was hair? And like maybe the moonlight was making a streak —"

"But then what about Buster?"

"*What* about Buster?"

"He kept an eye out and Hench didn't move."

"Buster," she said, "is a known gambler. I hate to say it but—"

"Right. Then don't."

For a time we were silent.

Sue paced the counter. I licked at my whiskers and chewed a few nails. "Okay, this is it," she said. "This is the answer. I know who's got him," she blurted. "Kent!"

"*Kent?*"

"The butler!" she said. "Oh Sammy, the butler did it!"

"The butler did *what?*"

"The butler," she said, "had a streak in his hair. You never saw him. You said so yourself. And he's working for Gutless, isn't he?"

"So?"

"So *Gut*less," she babbled, "sent Kent to get Louey when Jimmy told Gutless he'd bungled the job!"

I nodded discreetly. "Intelligent thinking."

"Oh, Sammy, really?" she beamed.

"But wrong. I mean, Louey was stolen while Jimmy was out. He was still like a dead man at way after two when I got to the alley, and Louey was gone. And he didn't call Gutless until he got home. But aside from *that*," I said, "nifty thinking."

Sue looked determined. "Then how about Jacques?"

I looked up at her wearily. "Why Jacques?"

"Did you ever see him?" she said. "You didn't. You never once got a look at his hair."

"Susie," I said, "there are millions of scalps that I haven't examined. Does that make them guilty?"

She glared at me greenly and snapped at me. "Yes!"

For a couple of seconds we glowered in silence. Then Sue threw her paws up and said, "I quit. This story is screwy," she sniffed. "I mean, it's got interesting characters, patches of wit, some intelligent dialogue, dozens of twists, but it doesn't make sense, Sam. The story's a mess and it doesn't make sense and it just never will."

"But it's got to," I told her.

"*Why?*" she said sharply.

"Because it's just got to. Let's try it again." I jumped to the sofa and stared at the ceiling. I started to picture the stuff that I'd seen. In Sebastian's pockets...

"Talk to me, Sammy. Say what you're thinking. Just say it aloud." She settled beside me and rested her chin on the edge of my shoulder. I patted her head. The radio blatted *My Favorite Things*. I tapped out the rhythm and thought about...things— the things that I'd looked at, the stuff that I'd missed, and then, to be funny, I sang out the list.

> "Wallet with money,
> And Visa that's dented.
> Cell phone (a swell phone)"

She said, "You're demented!"

> "Ticket for speeding
> As though he had wings—"

"Sam? What's the subject? Sebastian?"

"His things."

"Oh," she said. "Well...was reciting them useful?"

"Nope. But the rhyming is quite Dr. Suess-ful."

"Mmm. And the rhythm's so cloying, it clings. So now do O'Shaughnessy's."

"Things?" I said.

"Things."

"Um...

> Letter from lawyer
> Evoking eviction.
> Ballpoints and car keys
> And unfinished fiction.
> Back of an envelope
> Covered with scrawls—"

"Stop!" she said.

"Why?"

"Cuz you'll never rhyme 'scrawls.' "

"My gosh," I said, "dozens of things rhyme with 'scrawls.' "

"But they'll never make sense!— Did you see any balls?" I shook my head no. "Did you see any shawls?"

"I didn't," I said.

"So there's walls and there's halls but then every apartment has walls and has halls. So I bet you can't rhyme it and stick to the theme."

I said, "What are we betting?"

She grinned at me. "Cream?"

"Against?"

"Well, against...that tonight we don't part."

"Done," I said speedily.

"Start from the start."

"Okay," I said, rapidly tapping my art:

> "Letter from lawyer
> Evoking eviction.

Ballpoints and car keys
And unfinished fiction.
Back of an envelope
Covered with scrawls—
That is the sum of what
Sammy recalls!"

"Oh, foo!" she said. "You did it. And it even makes perfect sense."

"Yes, it does," I said, "doesn't it." I stopped for a second and thought. "Oh my goodness," I said. "It does!"

I jumped to the carpet and raced for the door.

"Where are you going, Sammy?"

I looked at her. "Back to the office."

"You don't want your cream?"

"I'll come back for it later," I said, and went off.

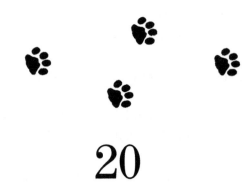

20

Click! Click! Ideas were colliding like balls on a pool table, moving so fast that I couldn't keep up with them. Pieces of puzzle were coming together and clicking their clicks and delivering pictures—pictures of car keys and letters from lawyers and tickets and pens. It didn't make sense—or it didn't completely. I needed more pieces to work the thing out but the first one was easy, or ought to be easy. I lived in a bookstore. I needed a book.

I was standing on tiptoe and looking at shelves when the back office telephone rang in the dark. I let it get answered by Hunnicker's voice and then waited tensely with ears cocked. Spike, in a whisper—a hurried rasp that meant Donna was coming or possibly there— said, "Sam, check your e-mail! I sent you some stuff."

I went back to the office and started the Mac. The only new message that waited was Spike's:

I did what you wanted. I checked
on Hench and endangered species.
Here are some links.

I looked at the list and then clicked on the first
one. *Wanted-catkillers.com*. The internet's something, isn't it? Name any weirdo subject, it's right
at your feet.

And there was my villain. Herman Hench, known
as Peter Patter and Jack Sprat, was wanted for killing Siberian tigers— endangered tigers so totally rare
there were maybe a hundred-and-twelve in the world,
and the sentence, per tiger, was seven years. Hench
was suspected of murdering two.

I learned that the sentences sprung from a law—
a world-wide agreement America'd signed in the
1970s— making a crime out of "capturing, killing,
collecting, importing, possessing or smuggling"
a long list of folks, from the elderly tortoise on
Gutless's floor to the elegant elephant, killed for its
tusks that were hung on his mantel.

I clicked on the link to *Endangered Strangers*.
The listing of creatures went on for a foot. Odd-look-
ing strangers I'd never heard of—komodo dragons
and Javan snails.

And then came the birds. I looked up at their
pictures, and matched all the parrots I'd seen in the
cages at Gutless's mansion with birds on the list.

My eyes grew wider. Tibetan Antelopes, used
to make blankets, or sweaters and shawls (or the
soft Gutless afghan I'd seen on his couch) were also
endangered and said to be worth about six hundred
thousand in dollars and cents and enough time in
prison to make you think twice about pulling the

111

wool off of somebody's back.

I thought for a second and scrolled to the top and confirmed that "possessing" was part of the crime.

I typed in *Gutless* and waited seconds and got to his bio, and started to laugh. I was hitting paydirt, at length and at last.

There was one other piece that was part of the puzzle. I knew where to find it. It's where I'd begun, in the depths of the bookstore. I raced to the shelves.

The book I was after was right in the O's:

MOONSHOT

The prize-winning novel
by
John D. O'Shaughnessy

At twenty of seven on Monday morning, I worked at the telephone, making the calls. I was calling a meeting for 8 PM. First I called Buster in Room Twenty and gave him instructions on how to proceed. Then I called Slasher at Healthier Pet. Then I called Spike with some further instructions, and waited till 7 to waken Jean-Clawed. I stared at the ceiling. That was my list. Spike would get Brigid at 7:30; Buster'd said Wilmer would be there on time.

I was racked from not sleeping. I'd read through the night and then shot off an e-mail and paced on the sill. I looked up at the sun rising gamely but weakly, and felt my exhaustion. I started to yawn. Then I went to Kaboodle, where Sue waited sweetly, and curled up beside her and slept like a dog.

21

The meeting had started like musical chairs. Jean-Clawed, it appeared, wouldn't sit next to Brigid; Brigid, in turn, wouldn't sit next to Wilmer; Wilmer had gawped for a second at Slasher and scuttled away like a little white mouse, and then Slasher had fled from the finicky Frenchman, —disliking his bow or his odor or both— and then everyone scrambled around in the office till Sue put a stop to it.

"*Stop it!*" she said.

Everyone stopped it and stayed where they were. Brigid and Spike settled down on the blotter, Sue on the table, Jean-Clawed on the sill, Wilmer alone on the edge of a bookshelf with Slasher above him, and me at the Mac.

Buster was late but I started without him.

Looking at Brigid, I said, "Here's the bit. We'll be playing a game and the game is called Truth. So if anyone lies, she gets twenty demerits and loses the kitten."

"The kitten?" she said. Her brow seemed to lift in suspicious surprise. "Oh Sam, do you have him? My sweet little Fluffer?"

"He isn't your Fluffer," Jean-Clawed nearly spat.

I said, "Everyone quiet and let's start the game. I'll begin with a story, and later I'll ask you to answer some questions. Is everyone in?"

Everyone nodded.

I started the game. "All right," I said, nervously tapping my tail. "On Friday, " I said, "in the afternoon, Mr. John O'Shaughnessy left his house at about— what time was it, Brigid?"

"Four." She looked up at me, frowning. "But why do you ask?"

I evaded her question. "What mood was he in?"

"He was terribly angry," she said.

"Uh-huh. I imagine he'd recently opened the mail."

Her blue eyes widened. "But how did you know?"

"He went out of the house with a piece of that mail, and with one other item. A ballpoint pen. He'd opened a package of three on the desk and took one of them with him."

She nodded slowly.

"You know what was in it? I mean, in the mail?"

She lowered her eyes. "An eviction notice."

"You know where he went with it?"

"*Sam?*" she pled.

"Just answer the question."

"He said on the phone he was seeing his landlord to argue his case."

"And who is his landlord?"

She mumbled, "You know."

"But I want you to tell me."

"It's...Caspar Gutless."

Everyone gasped and then started to talk. I looked quickly at Slasher. "The same Caspar Gutless who rents Jimmy's store to him. Fat Mr. G. He owns about seventeen blocks in the Village and finds it amusing to throw people out. It was all in his bio." I clicked on the site with the map of his holdings. "You see?" I said. "Look."

"Well, he ain't throwin *Jimmy* out." Slasher stood up and then raked at the air with a talon-like claw. Jean-Clawed shot a look at him. Slasher said slowly, "I'll eat all his ankles and chew off his nose."

"You'll do nothing but sit here," I told him, "now sit!"

Slasher looked at me sideways, but stayed where he was. I swiveled to Wilmer. "At four on Friday, you still lived at Gutless's."

"Yeah. That's right."

"You remember what happened there?"

Wilmer nodded. "A fella come over and brought him the rug."

"The Siberian tiger."

"Whatever," he said. "But the fella come early. He's not expected. He's s'posed ta deliver it way after dark, only Gutless don't argue, you know what I mean? Like he gets all excited. He's nuts for the rug."

"And you know who the 'fella' was?"

"Guy named Hench."

"A guy who's wanted," I told him, "for trapping and trading in animals."

Wilmer looked dim. "So what?" he said carelessly. "What's it to *me?*"

115

I said, "You're an animal, Wilmer."

"Yeah? Come out in the alley and say that again."

Spike started laughing. "The point was just proved.—Get on with the story, Sam. What happened then?"

"Then the two of them walked into Gutless's office. They started talking and bolted the door." I looked up at Wilmer who angled his head.

"You been spyin' or somethin'?"

"I gather, Monsieur, he's been using his talent to figure it out." Jean-Clawed made a wink at me. "Please to go on."

"So they're locked in the office," I said, "and they talk. And *then* what, Wilmer?"

"This other guy comes. So Kent does his Brit-thing, you know what I mean? Like 'The Mah-ster is busy and kahnt be disturbed.' So the guy don't like it. He says, 'I just called and he told me he'd see me.' He's ticked as a clock. So Kent does his Brit-thing again and this other guy muscles on past him and runs up the stairs. So Kent follows after and sits the guy down."

"In the room with the sofa," I said. "The room that's in front of the office."

"So how'd you know *that?*"

"Well I didn't exactly," I said. "Except that his idiot ballpoint was under the couch. And it started to figure."

Spike cocked his head. "I don't get this at all," he said. "*What* figured?"

"That Mr. O'Shaughnessy had to be *there*. That he had to have heard when the kidnap was planned. And Gutless admitted he planned it with Hench on

116

Friday at 'tea-time,' whatever that means, and I figured it means about quarter-to-five. The office was closed but the voices carried. O'Shaughnessy heard them, and even made notes. On the back of his envelope. Using his pen. At some point or other, he got an idea and he got up abruptly—dropping his pen—and he hurried on out of there. Then he went home—"

"He got home at five-thirty-ish," Brigid agreed.

I grinned at her. "Thank you. I think that's the truth."

"And *then* what happened?" Sue was all ears. "My goodness, Sammy. So what happened then?"

"Then..." I said vaguely. "Then...I'm not sure."

"Then he called Information," Brigid chimed in. "And he asked for the number of Beaumont Nursery, but something was wrong with it. Some kind of voice said the phone wasn't working, the circuits were down. And he slammed down the phone and he started to pace. He kept pacing and pacing. First he was frowning and then he was laughing. He gave me a kiss and said, 'Brigid, Brigid, you live with a genius!' And then he was cackling and then he said 'Wow'—"

"—and he picked up his car keys and raced from the house."

She nodded prettily.

"What was the time?"

"It was six twenty-seven."

"And how do you know?"

"There's a nice little clock in the VCR. It's across from the sofa, and that's where I was."

"Did you know where he went to?"

She shook her head no. "I had no idea where he went to at all. Oh I know what you're getting at, Sam. You've decided he went to the Nursery and stole little Fluff. But I'll never believe that. He isn't a thief."

"And yet he returned around one in the morning and brought little Louey."

She nodded again.

There were more exclamations and noise from the crowd.

"It was Saturday morning," she said, "when I woke. So I can't say for certain what time he arrived. But he did have the kitten. This wonderful beautiful little black fluffer asleep on his bed."

"So it *was* O'Shaughnessy." Sue clapped her paws. "But then how did Sebastian—"

"I'm getting there. Wait." I paced on the blotter and turned to Jean-Clawed. "You told me Sebastian departed New York at about seven-thirty."

"Exactly, Monsieur."

"And you'll stick with the timing?"

"I certainly will. The radio said so, Monsieur. Though I rarely believe in their weather, they do know the time."

I looked over at Wilmer. "So what about Hench?"

He looked back at me stupidly. "*What* about Hench?"

"The subject," I said, "is what time did he leave?"

"You expect me to *know* that?" He glared at the crowd. "What's *wrong* with you people? You sit watching clocks? You know that it's seven-oh-one when you're hungry and seven-oh-two when you finish your food?"

118

Brigid glowered right back at him. "La-dee-dah! And I bet you don't even know how to tell time."

"I can tell that the rug merchant left before dinner!"

"And what time is dinner?" I said.

"Six o'clock!"

"All right. There we have it. It's just as I thought. It's a three-hour drive to the Beaumont Nursery. Hench must've gotten there, say about nine and staked out the Nursery, planning to strike. Only while he was waiting, O'Shaughnessy entered. O'Shaughnessy left as Sebastian arrived—"

"Only hold it a second!" Spike waved his paw and then frowned concentration and looked at Jean-Clawed. "It was seven-thirty, you said, when he left. That's a whole hour later than everyone else. So explain to me, Sammy. You're saying O'Shaughnessy took a whole hour to kidnap the kid?"

"But Sebastian was speeding," I said. "Remember? He got that ticket at three-before-ten and he got it in Wigham, a mile from the farm. But forget about numbers. The point would be this: That Sebastian Beaumont saw John O'Shaughnessy stealing the kitten. Or thought that he did. So he made a U-turn and followed him home and then Hench, observing it, followed them both."

"Like he followed Sebastian who followed O'Shaughnessy?" Spike wasn't happy.

"It has to be so. It's the one explanation that makes any sense."

"*Sense?*" Sue was angry. "It doesn't make sense."

"It does if you'll listen," I said.

She glared.

119

I paced on the blotter some more and looked at the deadpan faces that circled my path. They neither believed me nor disbelieved me. They simply waited. I sighed and went on.

"So the two of them parked at O'Shaughnessy's curb and they stared at his windows. Hench is a pro, so he must have been careful. I'd bet Sebastian remained unaware of him.— Brigid—you're on. What happened on Saturday?"

"Nothing at all. What I mean is, O'Shaughnessy slept until noon and then wrote like a blue-streak till way after dark and I played with the kitten. After a while, we were all getting hungry—at seven-oh-six—" she looked bullets at Wilmer— "and just about then is when Mr. O'Shaughnessy went to the store."

"And when Jacques and Sebastian," I said, "broke in."

Jean-Clawed grew indignant again, a thing that he did very nicely, with Gallic aplomb. He jutted his jaw out and looked down his nose. "I would beg your *pardon*, Monsieur. And I'd ask you to tell me how Jacques was a part of this plan."

"He was driving the truck that said 'Beaumont Gallery'. The way I figure, Sebastian phoned him, using the cell phone I found in his coat. Sebastian was sitting there, stuck in his car and watching O'Shaughnessy's, hour after hour, and he phoned up his brother and said, 'Come and help.'— Can you prove something different?"

His jaw went down and his eyes went with it. "Alas, Monsieur. If I have to be honest, I'd tell you truly that Jacques got a phonecall and left in a rush. It was most unusual. Closing the store in

120

the middle of Saturday, taking the truck..." He looked up at me fleetingly, shaking his head.

"They got in through the door," I said, "using the trick of inserting a credit card into the lock. It's an old-fashioned lock and it's easily sprung, but Sebastian's Visa card seemed to get bent, which is how I discovered it. Kindly remember," I added, "that Hench had been watching it all."

"I see what you're getting at." Spike looked alert. "So he saw them take Louey and leave in the truck and he followed the truck till it got to the Gallery. That explains everything! Then he broke in and the rest would be history!"

"Well, not quite. There's the whole second half of it. Everything else has—"

A sudden commotion arose from the store. The clang of the mail slot, the clatter of feet, and a babyish mewing as Buster appeared with the little black kitten on top of his back.

22

He knelt down gently and lowered the kid. "He was just where you said he was, Sammy. And, boy, what a great little jockey." He beamed at the kid. "If you had a real horsey, you'd win at the Derby." From under the lamplight, the kitty-cat blinked and said "Horsey, Horsey!" and giggled and yawned. Brigid had pounced on him, licking his face. "Why the baby is freezing!" she hollered at Buster. "Why, what were thinking of, dragging him out? Oh my sweet little Fluffer," she cooed, "Are you cold?"

She attempted to warm him by pulling him closer. The kitten giggled again and said, "Mom," and then snuggled right into her, Sue, going "Ooo," with that goofy expression that ladies adopt in the presence of kids. Spike looked impatient and groaned in his throat. Slasher was squinting, Wilmer was bored, and Jean-Clawed was appraising the kitten like art.

"Monsieur will observe," he said, after a second,

"the family resemblance in whiskers and claws and the quite unmistakable Beaumont nose. I would know the child anywhere. This is my Louey, and now I shall claim him and bid you goodnight."

"Hold your horse and your kitten there, Frenchy!" Slasher was carefully rising to terrible heights. He loomed over everyone, casting a shadow that fell on the kitten. "I'm takin' the kid. Gotta have him so's Jimmy holds onto his store."

Wilmer looked at him slyly. "So figure me in. I could worm my way back into Gutless's mansion, accounta I helped you deliver the kid."

They leapt for the kitten. I leapt for the gun. It was Jean-Clawed's pistol, the one that I'd hid, with its ink supply dribbling and ready to shoot. I aimed at the desk top and said, "Hold it there!"

Everyone froze and then sucked in their breaths. I felt pretty stupid there, aiming that pistol. I wouldn't have shot it, I wouldn't know how, but it seemed to discourage immediate plans. "Now back away from him. Nice and slow."

They backed away from him. Nice and slow.

Buster, who'd risen to cover the kid, gave a nod of approval. Spike looked relieved.

"Now let's just relax." I looked up at Jean-Clawed. "And let's talk about lobster."

Sue made a gasp.

Jean-Clawed looked embarrassed. "I know I promised you five pounds of lobster, Monsieur, but, alas, I am presently fishless. The most I could raise would be two cans of tuna."

"That wasn't the deal. Nonetheless, go and raise them," I said. "Go on. I won't give the kitten to anyone else, at least not while you're absent."

He shot me a look of mistrust and suspicion but left for the door.

I turned back to Sue who was busily glowering. "They dyed the kitten," I said. "Tell me how. You're the expert groomer."

"I'm expert enough that I'd never dye one," she said. "He'd die. A cat licks his fur and he'd start to get poisoned. I guess the trick would be natural dye, and the only *black* dye I ever heard of is made out of caviar, olives and squid."

"And how long would it last, in your expert opinion?"

"A couple of weeks," she said. "Maybe a month. But of course if you washed him, the color would fade."

"So then why don't you wash him and see what you get."

Brigid said, "*Water*? You'd wash him with *water*?" She cuddled the kitten, who'd fallen asleep, but she held him protectively.

Sue made a face. "The water won't kill him. Honestly, Brigid, we'll do it together with nice warm—."

"*Please!* Just don't say the *word* again!." Brigid looked frantic and highly unhappy and covered her ears.

Spike whispered softly, "I'd do what he says. Like we'd need to be certain," he said, "that it's Louey and not some imposter—you see what I mean?"

Sue got excited. "Because if he *isn't*, then Brigid could keep him. Is that how it goes?"

I said, "Anything's possible, isn't it?"

124

"Oh." Brigid looked at me hopefully.

"Out with you, ladies. Get on to Kaboodle and into that sink."

I waited as Brigid, still half-reluctantly, lifted the kid by the nape of his neck and then carried him tenderly out through the store, with Sue tailing after her.

Slasher looked mad. "If this is a stall—" he said, swallowing hardware.

"You want to bring Jimmy the wrong little kid? It'll make Gutless madder."

Wilmer was giggling. "You can't make him madder, he's already *nuts*."

"Then why," Buster said, "would you want to go back there?"

"Well...I wouldn't. Except for the food. Like the food there is excellent."

"Yeah, but I bet that he doesn't have roaches and fat little mice."

"Gee, you got roaches?" Wilmer looked up, like he might reconsider as Spike scratched his jaw.

"Would you kindly continue," he said to me. "Please? I mean finish the story. So what happened then?"

I said, "Where was I?"

"It's Saturday night," Spike prompted helpfully. "Hench shot Sebastian and left with the kid."

"And went off to the Pearl," Buster added.

"And ordered a bottle of Hennessey," Wilmer threw in.

"And got up to his bedroom and called Mr. Gutless. He said, 'I've got him.'" I grinned at the group. "And they made an appointment—or so I'd imagine—I'd guess for Sunday to transfer the kid—and then he hangs up and gets totally wasted. But here's what's important. He misses the news." I paced on the desk which was now less crowded with half of us missing. "The ten o'clock news that goes on about Louey and Louey's reward."

Buster said, "Listen—he couldn't've watched it, he'd wanted to watch it. The set doesn't work."

"Only Gutless watched it. Ten o'clock comes and he's watching the newscast in total surprise. He's already got it that Hench has the kitten, but now he gets worried. Supposing that Hench gets a load of the bounty— the fifty thousand— and turns in the kitten, or raises the price. So he tries to get cutesy and hires Jimmy." I turned to Slasher. "He goes to the store. You said he arrived about ten to eleven?"

Slasher just nodded and watched me with awe.

"And he tries to buy Jimmy for two-hundred bucks and a hard luck story. And Jimmy goes out and gets hit by some lumber and Louey escapes."

"Only somebody rescues him," Buster said quickly. "A good-lookin guy with a streak on his head." He looked up at me, grinning. "And Sam got it right. He was just where you said he was, Sammy. Happy and safe and asleep on a corduroy couch."

"*Will you please give the answer?*" Spike was as ticked as I've ever seen him. "*You're driving me nuts.*"

"Roll it back for a second. To Saturday night. Mr. John O'Shaughnessy comes through his door with a bundle of groceries and what does he find?"

"That there isn't a kitten." Spike made a shrug.

"And there isn't a Brigid," I said. "She's gone.

126

She'd gone to the Gallery. I'd have to imagine she looked in the phonebook and found the address."

"Really rub that in." Spike was deeply embarrassed but trying to hide it by shooting me looks.

"So he went out to hunt for them. That's what he did. Taking Brigid's carrier. Roaming the streets until well after midnight. That's when he stumbled on poor little Louey and took the kid home. Or so I'd imagine."

"But how did you know? I mean how did you know he's the guy with the streak?"

"There was something that bothered me, Spike. From the start." I looked over at Slasher and said, "It was you. You were watching O'Shaughnessy's Saturday night. You were there when I got there. Why were you there?"

"Because—"

"No, don't tell me," I said, "let me guess it. You'd followed Jimmy. You'd wanted to help him or maybe protect him. He left for the Pearl and you followed right after him. Saw the whole thing. Saw him hit by the lumber and then saw O'Shaughnessy taking the kitten, and followed him home."

Slasher said, "Pally— ya got my respect."

"And there's one other factor," I added, and opened the copy of *Moonshot* I'd left on the desk. O'Shaughnessy's picture was slapped on the flap. He was handsome, all right, and his jet black hair had a big streak of white in it, right at the top.

"So you're not such a genius then." Wilmer looked smug.

"I wouldn't be sure of that," Buster threw in as the traveling Frenchman showed up with the cans.

127

23

It was Bumble Bee tuna, the solid white in the 3-ounce cans with the pop-top lids, very carefully wrapped in a plastic bag that he rakishly dangled between his teeth. Jean-Clawed set it down and said, "Where's the kitten?"

"He's getting a bath," I said, "right next door."

"An actual *bath?*" he said. "Bath with *water?*"

I nodded grimly. "It had to be done."

Jean-Clawed seemed to shudder. "I do see your point. We would have to attempt to return him to gold, but it seems such a torture for one so young. An actual *bath,*" he said, shaking his head. He flicked at the tuna. "Monsieur, I beg you to take this tuna as simply a gift, an additional bonus to cover your time and your personal genius. The lobster will come—on my word of honor— in less than a week."

"I prefer to do business," I said, "C.O.D."

"You would rather have *cod* than a beautiful lobster?"

I looked at him flatly and said, "Never mind." I tapped on the novel. "Has anyone read it?" I looked at the faces; I'd picked the wrong group. "It's an excellent story," I said. "The book's about stealing a necklace and pulling a—"

"Sam! Sam! *Sam!*" Sue arrived in a hurry, followed by Brigid with kitten in mouth. "He isn't Louey! He couldn't be Louey!" They leapt to the blotter and, very gently, Brigid set Louey (or Fluffer) to rest on the top of the novel. The kid looked cranky and terribly sleepy and...totally black. In fact, even blacker because he was clean. He shone in the lamplight, as perfectly burnished as natural ebony. "Look," she said, "See?"

Jean-Clawed was astonished. "There must be an error. Or possibly somebody—" glancing at Brigid— "decided to switch him with some little mutt."

"Oh somebody switched him, all right." I looked at the circle of faces. "You want to know who? Algernon Beaumont. That's who switched him. And John O'Shaughnessy cooked up the plot. It's the plot of *Moonshot*," I said to them. "Practically down to the commas." I tapped at the book, which disturbed little Fluffer, who started to mew. Brigid cradled him tenderly.

Slasher was mad. "I'm beginning to hate this," he said. "I am totally hating this story."

I grinned at him, "Don't. There's a wonderful ending— for everyone here."

"Yeah? How does *that* go?" Slasher was tense and ready to rumble.

Buster said, "Hey! Just cool it and listen." He turned to me. "How?"

"Because Algernon Beaumont still has the kitten. He never lost him. Louey's at home.—And your handsome roommate," I babbled to Brigid, "is really a genius and isn't a thief."

"But I always knew that," she said. "He lies and he makes up stories, but that's what he does."

"Like you mean he writes fiction," I said.

"And *fiction*," she said with conviction, "is nothing but lies. Like you make up a story and then you get paid."

"And he made up a winner," I said to her. "Listen. The plot he concocted went something like this: In exchange for alerting the Beaumont family to Caspar Gutless's hideous plan, he suggested they join him in pulling a switch. They'd pretend that the kitten was actually missing. They'd call up the papers and post a reward. Then a day or two later, O'Shaughnessy figured, he'd bring little Fluffer to Gutless's house and say he was Louey, and Louey'd been dyed, but the dye would grow out in a couple of weeks. In exchange for the kitten, he'd get Mr. Gutless to give him a lease for the next thirty years. And the lease would be binding, you see what I mean?"

"Oh I got it, I got it!" Spike was delighted. "A wonderful story. An excellent plot. And of course he'd have said it was permanent dye, so that Gutless would just have to wait and wait—"

"And wait and wait." Sue was dancing in circles.

"And wait and wait," Buster added, and laughed.

"Oh goodness, I love it!" Brigid was merry. "And meanwhile, of course, we'd be safe in our house like forever and ever." She cuddled the kid, and then suddenly darkened. "But hold it," she said. "If he actually *gives* little Fluffer to Gutless, I'll lose little Fluffer."

I said, "But you won't." I looked up at the clock. It was 9:17. "Because just about now," I said, "Sergeant Rafferty, Seventh Precinct, is raiding the house."

They looked up at me stupidly.

"*Gut*less's house. I sent him an e-mail," I said. "A strictly anonymous e-mail from Friend of the Cats. C'mere. Take a look at it. See what I mean?"

I pulled up the "sents" from my column of e-mails, and showed them the letter I'd written at dawn.

FROM: sam@samthecat.com
DATE: Monday, December 13, 5:27 AM (EST)
TO: Rafferty_JQ@7thPrecinct.com
SUBJECT: Dangerous Killer

Sgt. Rafferty:
Herman Hench, wanted for killing endangered species, will be at the mansion of Caspar Gutless on Monday evening at 9 PM. You will find all the evidence right in the mansion: the wanton destruction of rare species, the forced enslavement of rare birds. And the man who "possesses" them—Caspar Gutless —should also be busted, according to law.
Yours sincerely,
Friend of the Cats

"Oh Sam, that's sensational!" Sue was aglow. "And you're certain they're doing it?"

"Truly, for sure. I checked it with Gomez." I looked at Jean-Clawed. "So I owe him a dinner, and that's why I asked.—So is everyone happy?"

131

I looked at the crowd.

Brigid was frowning. Her blue eyes blazed. "So how does that help me?"

"Because," I said firmly, "with Gutless in jail for the next hundred years, you can keep your apartment *and* little Fluffer."

She thought for a moment and then she said, "Oh." And then she said, "*Oh!*" and then she said, "*OH!*" and enfolded the kitten as Buster looked on. He said, "Beautiful going." The kitten looked up and said, "Horsey, horsey," and then he said, "Dad?"

Brigid and Buster were suddenly glancing those mutual glances that sparkle with love and that never bode well for a gambler's future.

Slasher said suddenly, "Jimmy's okay? Like is that what you're saying?"

I nodded. "Uh-uh. So is everyone happy?"

They thought it over.

Wilmer checked Buster. "We really got bugs?"

Buster was nodding. Brigid was smiling. The kitten was purring. Jean-Clawed was content. Even Slasher was happy.

It started to snow.

24

It kept on snowing. Outside of my window, a giant pillow fight up in the sky kept delivering feathers that billowed and swirled. Sue sat beside me, the office empty except for the two of us, everyone gone. The only light was the screen of the Mac, where we'd captured an item from *Post Online* with its blistering headline:

MILLIONAIRE LANDLORD
BUSTED AT MANSION
CAT-KILLER HELD

"So everything's wonderful, isn't it, Sammy? Brigid gets Fluffer, and everyone's safe. What'll happen to Louey," she said, "do you know?"

I stared at the snowfall. "I guess he'll be fine. I'd imagine the Beaumonts'll phone up the press and say everything's settled and Louey's okay." I looked at her, shrugging. "His life'll be tough. There'll be cameras everywhere, dogging his trail. And he'll go to the cat shows and probably scream that his private dressing room isn't enough, and he'll win all the prizes—"

"And win all the girls."

"What a terrible life," I said. "Poor little kid."

She looked at me quizzically. "Tell me something."

"I'd rather be me and have you for a friend."

"That wasn't the question."

I said, "Don't worry, that wasn't the answer."

She glared at me. "Sam!"

"Go on. What's the question?"

"It's how did you know? I mean how did you figure that intricate plot?"

I said, "Maybe I didn't."

"*What?*"

"It's a plot, but I mean...who knows if it's really what happened? And then what's the difference? The bottom line is that everyone's happy and everyone's safe and the bad guys are punished. You add up the time for the tigers, the tortoise, the sheep and the birds—"

"And the rest of the cats—"

"And the elephant, too—and you're looking at centuries. Gutless and Hench'll be stuck in a cage like the cats in a zoo."

"That's poetic justice, isn't it?"

"Yeah."

We stared at the snowfall and stood very close.

"But what got you started?" she said.

"The things. And I put them together with something peculiar, something that practically slid past my ear. As Jean-Clawed told it, Sebastian came to—

134

after Hench stole Louey— and called up his dad. He said, 'Pops, I found Louey but somebody grabbed him,' and Algernon screamed at him, 'Get yourself home!' Plus he called him an idiot. See what I mean?"

"Like if Louey was missing—*actually* missing— he would've said 'Stay there and follow it up' and not called him an idiot."

"That's what I mean. And I'd figure that Fluffer was some kinda farm kid and easy to part with to pull off the switch. And there's one other thing, Sue. The paper reported that several cars had left tracks at the scene."

Sue thought it over. "I still think you're something." She started to yawn at me. "Brilliant and great."

She curled up beside me and looked at the snow, which was nearly hypnotic. The whirling, twirling, curling, hurling of feathery snow. I pictured the tiger, who rose from the dead, repossessing his spirit— his sinew and bone—and escaped from the mansion, his eyes like lanterns that broke through the darkness and burned his way home. I pictured him free and entirely happy—alive and alone on a whitening plain, his whiskers frosted, his luminous eyes on the Asian horizon, his mate in the cave. And for only a moment, I *was* the tiger. I felt his anger. I felt his pride.

Then I caught my reflection: a two-foot house cat in front of a window.

I looked down at Sue. For a two-foot house cat, I did pretty well.

About the Author

LINDA STEWART HAS WRITTEN 17 ADULT CRIME NOVELS AND FILM NOVELIZATIONS PLUS TELEVISION DRAMAS AND DOCUMENTARIES. *SAM THE CAT: DETECTIVE*, HER FIRST BOOK FOR CHILDREN, WAS INSPIRED BY HER LIVE-IN CAT, NAMED SAM, WHO GENEROUSLY LETS HER SHARE HIS MANHATTAN APARTMENT. THE FIRST BOOK IN THE SERIES (THAT NOW NUMBERS THREE) WAS NOMINATED FOR THE MYSTERY WRITERS OF AMERICA'S EDGAR AWARD.

About Sam

YOU CAN READ AN INTERVIEW WITH SAM HIMSELF (CONDUCTED BY GINGER PEACH, THE FELINE ASSOCIATE EDITOR OF *CATALOG* MAGAZINE) IF YOU GO TO SAM'S WEBSITE, WWW.SAMTHECAT.COM. HE WELCOMES QUESTIONS FROM READERS AND YOU CAN E-MAIL HIM THROUGH HIS SITE, OR WRITE TO HIM CARE OF THE PUBLISHER.

TO GET PERSONALLY AUTOGRAPHED COPIES
OR TO LEARN WHEN SAM'S NEXT BOOK WILL BE AVAILABLE
send a letter or postcard to
Cheshire House Books
P.O. Box 2484, New York City, NY 10021
or look for Sam's website:
HTTP://WWW.SAMTHECAT.COM

CPSIA information can be obtained
at www.ICGtesting.com
Printed in the USA
BVHW03s1731090918
526966BV00001B/47/P